AMERICAN HOUSEWIFE

Eating the Cheshire Cat: A Novel

AMERICAN HOUSEWIFE

· STORIES ·

Helen Ellis

DOUBLEDAY

NEW YORK LONDON TORONTO

SYDNEY AUCKLAND

This is a work of fiction. Names, characters, places, and incidents either are the product of the author's imagination or are used fictitiously. Any resemblance to actual persons, living or dead, events, or locales is entirely coincidental.

Copyright © 2016 by Helen Ellis

All rights reserved. Published in the United States by Doubleday, a division of Penguin Random House LLC, New York, and distributed in Canada by Random House of Canada, a division of Penguin Random House Canada Ltd., Toronto.

www.doubleday.com

DOUBLEDAY and the portrayal of an anchor with a dolphin are registered trademarks of Penguin Random House LLC.

Page 189 constitutes an extension of this copyright page.

Jacket design by John Fontana
Jacket photograph © Andrew McLeod / Trunk Archive;
floral print © Woodhouse / Shutterstock

LIBRARY OF CONGRESS CATALOGING-IN-PUBLICATION DATA
Ellis, Helen.
American housewife / Helen Ellis. — First edition.
pages ; cm
ISBN 978-0-385-54103-9 (hardcover)
ISBN 978-0-385-54104-6 (eBook)
I. Title.
PS3555.L5965A8 2016
813'.54—dc23
2015021779

MANUFACTURED IN THE UNITED STATES OF AMERICA

First Edition

1 3 5 7 9 10 8 6 4 2

For Ann Napolitano and Hannah Tinti,

great writers and friends

And I'm giving you a longing look
Everyday, everyday, everyday I write the book

—ELVIS COSTELLO

· CONTENTS ·

AMERICAN HOUSEWIFE

WHAT I DO ALL DAY

I nspired by Beyoncé, I stallion-walk to the toaster. I show my husband a burnt spot that looks like the island where we honeymooned, kiss him good-bye, and tell him what time to be home for our party.

I go to the grocery store and find that everyone else has gone to the grocery store and, as I maneuver my cart through Chips and Nuts traffic, I get grocery aisle rage. I see a lost child and assume it's an angry ghost. Fearing cold and flu season, I fist-bump the credit card signature pad.

Back home, I get a sickening feeling and am relieved to find out it's just my husband's coat hung the wrong way in a closet. I break into a sweat when I find a Sharpie cap, but not the pen. I answer my phone and scream obscenities at an automated call. I worry the Butterball hotline ladies are lonely. I follow a cat on Twitter and click "view photo" when a caption reads: "#YUCK." I regret clicking that photo. I weep because I am lucky enough to have a drawer just for glitter.

I shred cheese. I berate a pickle jar. I pump the salad spinner like a CPR dummy. I strangle defrosted spinach and soak things in brandy. I casserole. I pinwheel. I toothpick. I bacon. I iron a tablecloth and think about eating lint from the dryer, but then think better of that because I am sane. I rearrange furniture like a Neanderthal. I mayonnaise water rings. I level picture frames.

I take a break and drink Dr Pepper through a Twizzler. I watch ten minutes of my favorite movie on TV and lipsynch Molly Ringwald: "I *loathe* the bus." I know every word. *Sixteen Candles* is my *Star Wars*.

I hop in the shower and assure myself that behind every good woman is a little back fat. I cry because I don't have the upper-arm strength to flatiron my hair. I mascara my gray roots. I smoke my eyes. I paint my lips. I drown my sorrows with Chanel No. 5.

At the party, I kiss my husband hello. I *loathe* guests who sneeze into the crooks of their elbows. I can't be convinced winter white is a thing. I study long-married couples and decide that wives are like bras: sometimes the most matronly are the most supportive.

I feign interest in skiing, golf, politics, religion, owl

collections, shell collections, charity benefits, school fund-raisers, green juice, the return of eighties step classes, the return of nineties grunge, a resurgence of bridge clubs, and Ping-Pong mania.

I say, "My breath is the Pinot Grigio-est."

I say, "I am perfectly happy not being a Kennedy."

I say, "I'd watch a show called *Ghost Hoarders*. Why is that not a show?"

I say, "You can take your want of a chocolate fountain and go straight to hell."

I see everyone out and face the cold hard truth that no one will ever load my dishwasher right. I scroll through iPhone photos and see that if I delete pictures of myself with a double chin, I will erase all proof of my glorious life. I fix myself a hot chocolate because it is a gateway drug to reading. I think I couldn't love my husband more, and then he vacuums all the glitter.

THE

WAINSCOTING WAR

From: Angela.Chastain_Peters@smythe-peterspartners.com
Cc: Robert.Peters@smythe-peterspartners.com
To: GailMontgomery54@yahoo.com
Subject: Thank you
Date: May 6, 2015 9:24 PM

Hi neighbor! Thank you for the welcome gift basket you left outside our apartment door. My husband and I don't eat pineapples because my life coach has us on an all-protein diet, but we appreciate the gesture. We gave the pineapples to the super, who said he'd ask his wife to ask you for your recipe for pineapple-glazed ham. Apparently you make one every Easter that makes the elevator shaft smell like a barbeque. WOW!

I've returned your basket to our shared mail table,

which I believe is an antique toilet. Might I take this opportunity to discuss remodeling our common hallway? Here's an idea: wainscoting!

From: GailMontgomery54@yahoo.com

To: Angela.Chastain_Peters@smythe-peterspartners.com

Re: Thank you

Date: May 7, 2015 6:25 AM

Dear Ms. Chastain-Peters,

The former resident of your apartment, Mrs. Giles Everett Preston III, and I remodeled our common area two years ago. I am sure you recognize her name from her generous endowments to public television and the Feline Rescue Society. She was a woman of impeccable taste. She imported our vintage wallpaper from France and the art and antiques were from her Pennsylvania estate.

When she passed away on your kitchen floor, she willed me the contents of our hallway. Needless to say, I am sentimentally attached to these treasures, especially to my sewing machine table that you have mistaken for a commode.

Co-op rules dictate that residents of both apartments

must contractually approve common area changes. In honor of my dear departed friend, I wish to keep the hallway in its current condition.

Sincerely,
Gail Montgomery

From: Angela.Chastain_Peters@smythe-peterspartners.com
To: GailMontgomery54@yahoo.com
Re: Thank you
Date: May 7, 2015 11:12 PM

Hi Gail! Call me Angela! Let's do away with the formalities and antiques that 100-year-old socialite widows like Mrs. Preston held so near and dear! Just because life-size oil paintings of Biblical slaughter are framed in gold doesn't mean they're in good taste. Our hallway looks like a room at the Met that makes schoolchildren cry.

As I'm sure you know, Mrs. Preston left every room of our apartment lined with wallpapers like the flocked purple damask in our shared hallway (along with MOUNTAINS OF CAT HAIR to which my husband is DEATHLY ALLERGIC). What you might not know is that wallpaper PEELS. I gave a corner above your door a tug so you can see how easily it comes off.

Mrs. Preston had tacked every peeling high corner in our apartment with balled-up Scotch tape. As our realtor told us, it's no wonder she fell off a stool and broke her neck.

Anyhoo, now all our walls are painted with what Benjamin Moore calls "New Beginnings" beige, and isn't that name apropos of yours and my burgeoning relationship? I have a few pails of New Beginnings left over—so that will cut down on our shared remodeling cost—and my husband and I feel so strongly about wainscoting that we're willing to pool our dual income from Smythe & Peters to foot that expense too. My life coach says that money can't buy everything, but two lawyers in one family can convince people it can!

Case in point: when we modernize the design of our shared hallway, you can take Mrs. Preston's art and antiques to enjoy in your own home! That vase could hold loose change. And while you're at it, why not put the sewing machine table to use and spruce up your wardrobe? Forgive me for being less than tactful, but long gone are the days of *Dynasty* shoulder pads and madras plaid.

Why don't you come over for a drink and you can see the wainscoting we had installed in our apartment for yourself. With a glass of Chardonnay and a tour I'll bet I can sway you! Shall we say tomorrow night after my husband and I get home from work around 7:00?

From: GailMontgomery54@yahoo.com

To: Angela.Chastain_Peters@smythe-peterspartners.com

Re: Thank you

Date: May 8, 2015 9:25 AM

Dear Ms. Chastain-Peters,

Thank you for the invitation, but I must decline. I do not drink and I cannot be swayed. Moreover, in my home, 7:00 p.m. is feeding time. Along with the vase and paintings, which are indeed museum quality, I inherited Mrs. Preston's foster cats. I myself am widowed twice and Wynken, Wolf Blitzer, Dodo, and Fred offer me great solace and companionship as long as I adhere to their feeding schedule.

It breaks my heart to hear what you have done with my dear friend's showplace. Mrs. Preston had character and the only thing with less character than Chardonnay is wainscoting. Mrs. Preston always said that wainscoting is the first sign of new money and an interior designer's most efficient way of inflating a bill.

Believe me (despite the financial benefits that come with sleeping with your boss and somehow getting that boss to break up his marriage to marry you), once you are widowed you will understand the value of saving a dollar. Imagine coming home from your husband's funeral to find yourself forever alone, bereft, and pacing circles within your wainscoted room while clad in dungarees so tight I'm surprised your legs don't ignite when they rub together. It is not a pretty picture, is it? It does not make my paintings of pyres and snake pits look so bad, does it?

Regarding your vandalism, I expect you to hire a professional contractor to repair the damage done to my wallpaper within the week. When I am satisfied that it has been restored to its original pristine condition, I will return your doorknob and number.

Sincerely,
Gail Montgomery

From: Angela.Chastain_Peters@smythe-peterspartners.com

To: GailMontgomery54@yahoo.com

Re: Thank you

Date: May 8, 2015 9:45 AM

You stole our doorknob?

From: GailMontgomery54@yahoo.com

To: Angela.Chastain_Peters@smythe-peterspartners.com

Subject: Noise disruption and further damage

Date: May 9, 2015 10:35 PM

Ms. Chastain-Peters:

I will not tolerate loud parties, the decibels of which are drifting out of your apartment and into our shared hallway at this very hour of 10:35 p.m. on a Thursday. Wainscoting is not soundproof and I am a woman who needs her eleven hours of sleep.

Moreover, your entertaining is disrupting the sleep schedule of Mrs. Preston's foster cats. Believe me when I tell you that these are not animals you want to run into while you and your inebriated guests are spilling wine onto our shared carpet and you yourself are drawing a mustache on St. John the Baptist and what looks to be male genitalia next to the exquisitely tortured mouth of Joan of Arc.

If you think your defacement of Mrs. Preston's paintings will make me take them down, you are mistaken. Mrs. Preston always said that you teach a dog not to make a mess by rubbing her nose in it. Or you get cats. You, madam, are no cat.

To quote your graffiti: Suck it.

Gail Montgomery

From: Angela.Chastain_Peters@smythe-peterspartners.com

To: GailMontgomery54@yahoo.com

Re: Noise disruption and further damage

Date: May 9, 2015 10:59 PM

Fuck you.

From: Angela.Chastain_Peters@gmail.com
To: GailMontgomery54@yahoo.com
Subject: News
Date: May 10, 2015 5:55 PM

Hi Gail! Me again! Guess what? Thanks to our last e-mail exchange, which was "randomly" monitored by my law firm, I've been suspended from practicing law due to my use of "unprofessional language" and "questionable personal conduct."

Anyhoo, the good news is: I'll be home much, much, MUCH more than usual and I will refocus ALL of my efforts into convincing you that a hallway renovation is not only wanted by my husband and myself, it is WARRANTED. My life coach says that it's easier to ask forgiveness than permission. So please forgive me for taking a shit on your sewing machine table.

WAINSCOTING RULES!!!!!

From: Angela.Chastain_Peters@gmail.com

To: GailMontgomery54@yahoo.com

Subject: Get those cats out of the hallway

Date: May 13, 2015 9:54 AM

Gail, what have you done? I cannot believe what I'm seeing through my peephole are cats. They are WAY too big to be cats. One of them has so much fur I can't see its eyes. The brown one is DROOLING! They are sniffing my doorknob hole. I can feel their hot jungle breath on my bathrobe! If my husband comes home right now and survives his third heart attack from the shock, he will die from the cat hair! He is going to have to take the SERVICE ELEVATOR! How you've managed to keep those things from smothering you while you sleep is a miracle. It's amazing that the city we live in allows "pets" that belong in a sideshow, but makes it illegal for me to have a switchblade. Well let me tell you something sister, you are living next door to a lawbreaker. Get those cats out of our hallway and then get to vacuuming every stray hair that has clung to your high-piled carpet and god-awful wallpaper, or I will slip my hand into my pantie dresser drawer and pull out the silk pouch that doesn't hold potpourri. Tell me, which beast is your favorite? Wynken, Wolf Blitzer, Dodo, or Fred?

Please excuse typos as this was sent from my iPad

From: GailMontgomery54@yahoo.com

To: Angela.Chastain_Peters@gmail.com

Re: Get those cats out of the hallway

Date: May 13, 2015 10:09 AM

Dodo is the one that ate Mrs. Preston's face.

From: Angela.Chastain_Peters@gmail.com

To: GailMontgomery54@yahoo.com

Subject: Hallway remodeling

Date: May 14, 2015 3:34 PM

Well Gail, thanks to your cats it looks like a hallway restoration is finally in order. While you left your cats unattended in their "yard," they clawed your paintings to shreds, clawed out huge chunks of wallpaper, clawed up the carpet, clawed up our shared mail table, and broke your vase into a hundred pieces. Perhaps they should be euthanized.

Anyhoo, for your perusal, I've attached photos of wainscoting from our apartment. Please notice the New Beginnings beige that I still think would be a lovely alternative to what now looks like a crime scene. On the bright side, your cats' clawing uncovered beautiful hardwood floors, which I personally prefer to carpeting.

Have I mentioned recessed lighting? My life coach says wall sconces glow like the souls of the damned. Plus, those twenty-watt candelabra bulbs are impossible to replace and screwing in anything stronger will risk an electrical fire.

Please do let me know when you put the cats down. Seeing what they did to the hallway, I fear for my personal safety.

From: GailMontgomery54@yahoo.com

To: Angela.Chastain_Peters@gmail.com

Cc: Robert.Peters@smythe-peterspartners.com

Re: Hallway remodeling

Date: May 14, 2015 5:25 PM

Dear Ms. Chastain-Peters,

The Feline Rescue Society can attest to the fact that Mrs. Preston's foster cats were declawed as a stipulation of their adoption. I have taken the liberty of copying your husband on this e-mail exchange so that he may understand the magnitude of your actions.

Gail Montgomery

From: GailMontgomery54@yahoo.com
To: Angela.Chastain@gmail.com
Subject: My sympathies
Date: June 6, 2015 9:25 AM

Dear Angela,

I am sorry to hear from the super that you and your
husband have separated. He told me that he has been
forwarding your husband's mail to a hotel, but was not
sure what to do with yours as it was piling up on what
remains of our mail table. He said he has not laid eyes
on you in weeks. To protect your privacy, I told him that
I would hold your mail while you are traveling.

The super asked if you had gone to "Europe" as so
many wives in this building do when their husbands
desert them. "Europe" means plastic surgery, rehab,
or agoraphobia. The last of these options is the most
troubling because if your finances are strained, by
say extra housing, divorce lawyers, and a neighbor's
impending lawsuit, psychiatrists and psychological
drugs are unaffordable. And from what I understand
about life coaches, they don't cheer on crazy ladies who
don't pay their bills.

Do you know what happens to a mentally unstable
woman living alone in a two-bedroom apartment that
could be sold in this housing boom for above market

value? The co-op board gathers evidence that she is a danger to herself and evicts her.

Mrs. Preston always said if you are going to be a shut-in, find something to do. Mrs. Preston fostered cats. The woman who lived in your apartment before her ran a doll hospital. The woman before her wrote erotic novels under a man's name. Mrs. Preston and her predecessors did not leave your apartment for decades. Already, you have been missing for seventeen days. Seventeen years is just around the corner.

And I know you are in there. I can hear you making a smoothie.

My suggestion is that you overcome your debilitating depression by restoring our hallway decor. Gluing my vase back together should be fun, like a jigsaw puzzle. Trolling the Internet for duplicate out-of-print wallpaper to rehang, a scavenger hunt. Reweaving the wicker lid of my sewing machine table, meditative. And mending the paintings might make you feel like an artist yourself.

As a compromise, I am willing to agree to hardwood floors. Refinishing them will give you even more to accomplish.

Recovery is all about baby steps, Angela. Step into our hallway, you can step into the world.

Gail

From: GailMontgomery54@yahoo.com

To: Angela.Chastain@gmail.com

Subject: Kudos to you on the hallway clean up

Date: June 11, 2015 11:11 AM

Dear Angela,

I must admit that you have stripped the carpet and wallpaper better than any paid professional. There is not one dot of dried paste anywhere to be found, and believe me I checked with a magnifying glass and a flashlight. I assume that you have taken my antique sewing machine table, vase, and paintings into your apartment for repairs. You will need good strong sunlight for that and I will confess that in the past our hallway wall sconces have been a bit dim. But the current state is a safety hazard. Unlike Mrs. Preston's foster cats, I cannot see in the dark. Please return the lightbulbs.

Best,
Gail

From: Angela.Chastain@gmail.com

To: GailMontgomery54@yahoo.com

Subject: Safety Measures

Date: June 12, 2015 2:23 AM

Hi Gail! Please be advised that I have sealed off your front door using duct tape and my cold marital bed sheets, which I stitched together using none other than your antique sewing machine. Brace yourself: what I'm about to do will be DIRTY and LOUD.

From: GailMontgomery54@yahoo.com

To: Angela.Chastain@gmail.com

Subject: Wainscoting

Date: June 14, 2015 8:04 PM

Miss Chastain, I have heard of inflicting your bad taste on others, but to pry up our hallway floorboards and hammer them picket fence style into our walls to emulate wainscoting is absurd. You are deranged. I am releasing Mrs. Preston's foster cats into the wilds of our common area. I will stop feeding them, but they are hunters. Push your dresser in front of your door, but the cats will get past it. Brace YOURSELF: I trust they will not starve.

From: Angela.Chastain@gmail.com

To: GailMontgomery54@yahoo.com

Re: Wainscoting

Date: June 15, 2015 4:21 AM

You're wrong, Gail. I am the hunter. Peek out your peep-hole and count how many of your beasts are left. ZERO. One at a time, they trespassed over my property line and into my apartment. I had to defend myself. And, as you know, it's easier to fight one on one. I won't have to buy groceries for months. By the way, my offer still stands for that drink and a tour. You'll be amazed at what I've done with the place. I've repainted the New Beginnings wainscoting with what I'm calling "Tigers' Blood."

From: GailMontgomery54@yahoo.com

To: Angela.Chastain@gmail.com

Re: Wainscoting

Date: June 15, 2015 6:25 AM

I will meet you in the hallway at noon.

From: Angela.Chastain@gmail.com

To: Margot.Mulligan_Kramer@gmail.com

Subject: Welcome

Date: December 9, 2015 3:36 PM

Dear Ms. Mulligan-Kramer,

I hope that you and your family appreciate the welcome pineapple basket I left outside your door last week. When I moved into the building, the former resident of your apartment, Mrs. Gail Montgomery, left the same welcome gift for me. Since I have not received an acknowledgment of my gift, I will assume you are a busy woman and will leave well enough alone. I will, however, use this as an opportunity to address the subject of our common hallway.

Ours is a shared space and should be respected as such. When Mrs. Montgomery departed, she gave me permission to decorate our hallway as I saw fit. The wainscoting was put up at great personal expense. Twice already I have had to clean your bicycle scuff marks off the Benjamin Moore New Beginnings beige paint. The rug is one-of-a-kind, from a rare breed of wildcat, and should not be used as a drying pad for your open umbrellas.

What you might not know is that I run a mail-order taxidermy shop out of my apartment. It affords me a comfortable lifestyle, which I appreciate even more after my divorce. My life coach says taxidermy is the new decoupage. Mrs. Montgomery would disagree.

The former resident of your apartment disagreed with me about a lot of things, but learned to compromise. You can help by parking your bike in the bike room and by buying an umbrella stand. And please be mindful of the antique vase that sits upon our mail table. It is extremely fragile and nearly impossible to repair.

Sincerely,
Angela Chastain

DUMPSTER DIVING

WITH THE STARS

I'm in Rhinebeck, New York, to compete on *Dumpster Diving with the Stars*. It was my best friend Amy Madeline's idea. In the history of celebrity reality shows, there has never been a contestant who is famous for being an author. Between Amy Madeline and me, hers is the name everybody knows. Her books are pastel with shoes or purses on their covers. They are book club books. Beach books. Like some women produce babies, Amy Madeline has a book come out of her every year. I published one book, fifteen years ago, but it was a doozy. What they call a "cult classic." Meaning the book was odd, but identifiable, and is now out of print.

Amy Madeline said, "You get on the show, you get reprinted. You get readers interested in what you're working on now."

I said, "But I'm not working on anything now."

She said, "But you will be."

Amy Madeline's faith is unnerving. She's like a double-D battery pack jammed in the Baby This 'n That doll that is me. As long as I keep writing, she doesn't have to think about how hard the writing life can be. But it's really not that hard. You just have to do it, get it published, and do it again. Problem is: my last three novels lie dead in a drawer. I'm forty-five. Maybe it's not too late to find something else that I'm good at.

When I arrive at the Beekman Arms, the front desk clerk hands over an actual brass key with a plastic number dangling from the chain, says she googled me and bought my book off of Amazon for ninety-nine cents, and then says she's at the part where the main character purposely flunks out of school.

She asks, "Why would she do that?"

I have no idea why she would do that. It's been so long since I wrote that novel I'm shocked I can remember the character's name. I give the front desk clerk my pat line to questions about my work that I don't know the answer to.

I say, "You'll have to keep reading and see."

My roommate for *Dumpster Diving with the Stars* is Mitzy Rodgers, former *Playboy* playmate and live-in girlfriend of Hugh Hefner. On the show, there's always a Miss Something-or-Other or a kicked-out girl group singer or an actress who's known only for her hot tub scene. For Mitzy, this is the first time she'll be separated from her identical twin, Bitzy. All their lives, they shared everything from string bikinis to an eighty-year-old Sweet'N Low daddy to a secret twin toddler language.

Mitzy says, "Bitzy bah-knows bah-what I bah-feel before I bah-do."

I ask Mitzy if she and Bitzy believe in telepathy, but before she can answer, the cameraman and producer barrel in, apologize for being late, do not introduce themselves, clip wireless packs to my jeans and Mitzy's two-hundred-dollar sweatpants, and a mic to my bra strap. They tape Mitzy's mic to her skin because she is not wearing a bra. Her breasts sit on her torso like old-fashioned alarm clocks.

The producer asks me to ask Mitzy my question again. Everyone stares as I brace myself on the edge of the floral bedspread. The last time I spoke publicly was nine years ago at Amy Madeline's wedding. Then, I was told to "eat the mic." I lower my head like Dustin Hoffman in *Rain Man*.

"Mitzy, do you and Bitzy believe in telepathy?"

Mitzy blows a grape bubble with her purple bubblegum, pops it with her finger, winds the gum around that finger, and then waggles it, play-admonishing me. "You know we're not allowed to have smartphones."

The cameraman and producer do not react. They are seasoned professionals and are already making themselves invisible in this tiny room crowded with furniture. *Cardinal Reality Rule #1: Behind-the-scenes people stay behind the scenes.* They let that *Survivor* contestant fall face-first into his campfire. They let that *America's Next Top Model* virgin get drunk and "lose" her virginity.

What Mitzy is referring to is *Cardinal Reality Rule #2: Nobody gets a cell phone.* Technology makes games way too easy. We all remember how un-fun it was to watch the IBM computer wipe the floor with Ken Jennings on *Jeopardy!* Not to mention the fact that watching someone talk or text on TV is as boring as watching someone talk or text right in front of you.

I notice the empty wall sockets. The room phone and TV are gone. For our month of filming, we'll be entirely cut off from family, friends, and current events. I'm ashamed to admit that the last *New York Times* article I read was about bullfrogs. I regret that the last thing I said to my husband was: "You should read that piece about the bullfrogs." I want to call him and say, "I love you and I miss you already," but if I break my contract I'll be sued.

Mitzy confides in me (and the rest of the network affiliates) that Bitzy is in the hospital having corrective surgery for the reason their parents called her Bitzy to begin with. She whispers, "Navel enhancement."

"You mean," I marvel at Mitzy's breasts and plump lips, "now *that's* supposed to be bigger, too?"

"No, Hef wants her to have a pretty innie. Bitzy's belly button is an ugly outie. It's like a balled-up piece of rubber cement. When we did our centerfold, Hef made sure it was under a staple. At pool parties, he makes her cover it with one of those little round Band-Aids."

Mitzy, it turns out, always wanted to be a decorator. Her room at the mansion is minimalist. She explains, "No stuffed animals." She pulls down her sweatpants to show me her vagina, which she bedazzled herself.

Over the whir of zoom lenses, I tell her about my themed Christmas trees that, along with Amy Madeline's hundred thousand Twitter followers and Facebook campaign, helped earn me a spot on *Dumpster Diving with the Stars*. Every year, my husband and I have a big blowout party based on a new Christmas tree theme that I create from used ornaments I buy off eBay. This year is Under the Big Top (all circus), last year was Motion in the Ocean (all sea life), and the year before that was Fat Hos (all Santas). As Mitzy's eyes grow moist with amazement, I get that proud feeling I used to get when Amy Madeline drew a heart by a sentence in a first draft of one of my chapters.

Mitzy bestows what I will come to learn is her highest compliment: "Cute!" Really, she coos it, so it sounds more like "Cooooot!" She asks if she can come to this year's party, and when I say okay, Mitzy looks like she will burst out of her imaginary bra. She says she will wear her trapeze outfit for the occasion. She has a trapeze outfit. Mitzy herself looks like something I would hang on my tree. She is miniature, plastic, and kitschy. I wonder how someone so fake can be so pure. She might be the most undervalued thing I find on this show.

———

At three o'clock, all eight contestants assemble on the front porch of the oldest inn in the Hudson Valley, where George Washington slept and if he were alive today would jail Mitzy for indecent exposure.

Before us stands the host of *Dumpster Diving with the Stars,* Elvin Smalls, whom Amy Madeline and I call F'in Tiny because the camera never shows his feet. Like a toned, tanned, tinted troll under a bridge, F'in Tiny likes to point out competitors' weaknesses. Last season, he told Cynthia Nixon her throat was splotchy. And then he told her those splotches were hives. F'in Tiny wears a safari hat and a canteen strapped to his belt.

He asks us, "Are you ready to DUMPSTER DIVE?"

Mario Batali shouts, "Yeah!" He jumps in place when he says it, so when he lands the only sound is the reverberation of his Crocs on 245-year-old porch planks.

The rest of us aren't sure how to behave. The married Scientologist actors want to remain respectable. The sports figure is, let's face it, too cool. I assume Mitzy doesn't jiggle unless she gets paid. Me, when was the last time I raised my voice? Sure, I shriek when the toast pops out of the toaster, but I am not a joiner-inner.

F'in Tiny repeats, "I *said*, 'Dumpster divers, are you READY?' "

Behind F'in Tiny a producer resurrects the *Arsenio Hall Show* dog-pound fist spiral. Mitzy is too young for this reference and looks up because she thinks (as it happens on every episode of *The Bachelor*) that a helicopter is landing. Another producer mutely WOO-HOOs so the mics won't pick up his sound interference. Eight cameramen look annoyed that our lack of over-the-top enthusiasm is going to make the day run long.

So, I clap.

And all the other contestants clap along with me.

We are a mature, appropriately enthusiastic bunch.

F'in Tiny says, "For your first challenge you will have TWO hours and TWO HUNDRED dollars to scour this small AMERICAN TOWN. The WINNER's find will have the BIGGEST difference between what you pay for it and fair market value. With each challenge, these differences add up, and the contestant with the greatest overall difference wins the whole show. And, as always on *Dumpster*

Diving with the Stars, you do not have to spend anything. The MORE you save, the MORE your find will be worth. Winning is a matter of pride. You keep what you find and those finds will be featured in a three-page spread in *Better Homes and Gardens.*"

Last season's winner, Diane Keaton, displayed her eighteenth-century bowling pins on her bathroom windowsill, in a triangle shape around her *Annie Hall* Oscar.

Amy Madeline and I pored over the photo.

She'd said, "Maybe you'll find something worthy enough to be photographed next to a Pulitzer."

I'd said, "But I don't have a Pulitzer."

She'd said, "Maybe you'll find something that will inspire you to write something great."

F'in Tiny says, "ARE. YOU. READY? Dumpster divers?"

"Yeah!" A few of us join Mario. Me included. Except, I raise my voice to say "Yesssss" instead of "Yeah" so it's my *ssss* that lingers on the porch this time.

F'in Tiny says, "For this challenge, you will pair yourselves into TEAMS of TWO. BUDDY UP for bargaining! Starting, NOW."

Part of me wants to jump on John Lithgow's back and ride him like a bull into the antique china shop across the street. The man is well over six feet tall and built. He smiles down at the lot of us like the mother alien at the end of *Close Encounters of the Third Kind*. Verbena Barber, a wily woman from *Nightcrawlers* (a reality show about her husband and six earthworm-grubbing sons), grabs his wrist. Lithgow nods pleasantly at the brownness of her. Her shoes, skirt, and blouse, and her husband's humongous jacket look residually damp from her hill country. I've seen Verbena's show and know her teeth are rotten, but today her face is scrubbed and her long hair is parted down the middle. She beams at Lithgow and in that split second I see him recall what I recall from her show: her teapot collection. She inherited the teapots from a rich old lady she'd done the ironing for. When that rich old lady was dying, she told Verbena to pick any one thing out of her whole mansion as an inheritance. Verbena picked her teapots because they were painted with fairies and gnomes and one was shaped like a duck. Turns out they were by British artist Lucie Attwell and each worth a small mint. On *Nightcrawlers* Verbena's always interviewed with the polished row of teapots sitting high on a shelf in the background of her log cabin. Lithgow knows she's got a good eye. And now we all know it because the Emmy winner and Verbena take off running.

Mitzy and I do too. I don't know how long she's been holding my hand, but she's got me and we're going.

Looking over my shoulder, I see the other contestants, cameramen, and producers running away from us and into the center of town after Lithgow and Verbena, who are already out of sight and through the doors of that antique china shop I had my eye on. I hear the clap, clap, clap of Mario's Crocs and the click, click, click of the stilettos on the size ten feet of the tennis player with whom he's paired himself. They're running toward *another* antique china shop. The married Scientologist actors are running toward something called an antique *barn*. F'in Tiny is left alone on the inn porch and lights a cigarette. The fiery dot grows dimmer as Mitzy drags our crew into a ravine.

"Trust me," she says, "the best stuff is by the train tracks!"

By God, she is right. Ten minutes later, I spot two wooden nubs sticking out of a thatch of sopping matted leaves. Who knows how many decades the rocking horse has been here. From neck to tail, it is buried in the damp ground. Mitzy and I scavenge for empty cans to dig it out. The digging takes almost the entire allotted two hours. The rush and roar of each passing train sends us screaming away from the tracks. We slip on wet leaves every time we run. Mitzy loses two press-on nails.

With ten minutes to go, she and I carry the beast, which is large enough to take the weight of both of us, up the hill to the Beekman Arms. The other contestants have made it back in plenty of time and are sitting on the porch drinking punch spiked by our sponsor, Captain Morgan, to loosen their tongues. Picnic tables are set with cloth-covered objects, finds waiting to be revealed. F'in Tiny scrolls through his iPhone under a small open tent. Cameramen encircle the property. Producers nab hotel guests wandering through the set and get them to sign appearance waivers.

The odor of Mitzy and me stops everyone. Think of what a vase of water smells like when you pull out dead daisies. Now imagine that Mitzy and I have shoved our arms into a bathtub of that water, knelt in that water, and run our fingers through our hair with that water. Mitzy is entirely in terry cloth, the clothing equivalent of a sponge. The rocking horse is waterlogged, but it's held its shape and paint. My arms are breaking from the weight of it. A rhinestone slips down the inside of Mitzy's sweatpants leg and catches the porch lights. A buzzer sounds. We've reached the checkpoint in time. We use all our strength and what's left of our composure not to drop the rocking horse hard.

Lithgow breaks the stunned silence with what we all thought we'd have to wait until the end of the series for, and I'm sure the producers thought they would have to coax out of him. He shouts a variation of his catchphrase from *Third Rock from the Sun:* "It's GOR-geous!"

His saying it this early must mean he's blown away.

The local appraisers are too. The horse is from the early 1900s and valued at five grand.

F'in Tiny peruses the remaining entries with the appetite he'd have for warm egg salad. He interviews the tennis player and asks if she worries her stilettos slowed down her team.

She eyes his head like the yellow fuzz ball that it is.

Mitzy and I win.

———

At dinner on the glassed-in sun porch, Mario asks me why it's been so long since I've written a book. I cut the head off a butter swan, put the whole thing on a piece of roll, and then put that whole thing into my mouth. I let the butter dissolve. The fresh bread sticks to my teeth. I chew. Hold up a finger. I'll answer him, I'll answer him—just let me finish this bite. I keep chewing, hoping that he'll lose interest and ask Verbena for worm recipes, but Mario, who eats with large parties on a nightly basis, patiently stares at me until his focus draws the attention of everyone at the table. Five cameras crowd for my close-up.

I say, "I've been writing, I just haven't published."

"What's the difference?" asks the tennis player.

I say, "It's hitting a tennis ball against your garage door versus Wimbledon."

"You see there!" booms Lithgow. "That's writing!"

I want to crawl across the table and kiss him on the lips. I say, "Thank you," and bask in the genuine warmth of his gaze. This is what a happy person looks like. He's got his health, family, the respect of the Academy of Motion Picture Arts and Sciences, and he's comfortable enough to go on *Dumpster Diving with the Stars*. Me, I'm struggling.

My literary agent, Maxine Jaffe (seventy-something and still one of the biggest in the business), has been gracious enough to keep me on as a client even after she couldn't get publishers to pony up the most minuscule of advances for my last three novels, the subjects of which she has been less than thrilled about.

She says, "Doll, you wrote a plantation book when there were two other plantation books on the bestseller list. You wrote a book about kids who turn into cats, when vampires are still—God help us—the only thing anyone wants to read about. You wrote a book about a witch who infects her entire neighborhood with herpes. Herpes, Doll! Trust me, nobody wants to read about that. I'm telling you: three generations of women, that's what sells. And the three *A*'s: adultery, abortion, anorexia. Will you trust me, Doll? I'm begging you."

Amy Madeline writes about smart put-upon overweight women who sit in front of black-and-white movies on TV and eat ice cream straight out of the carton. Sometimes, they pour Froot Loops and milk into the half-empty carton. They have overbearing skinny mothers and wonderful drunk grandmothers. They have Spanx accidents. They learn that when they finally love themselves, men will too. Amy Madeline's books are hilarious and touching and I love that I get to read her first drafts before her initial print runs of 100,000.

Maxine says, "All these years with Amy Madeline at your side, I'd think her ideas would rub off on you."

That's the problem: once my best friend puts something in her books, I feel like I'm stealing if I put the same thing in mine. So far that rules out book clubs, cat lovers, art lovers, grandmas-gone-wild, cancer, child pageants, and murderous housewives. I can't write a book in e-mail format. I can't write a book in second person.

I've spent the last ten years coming up with the bizarre, while my real life has grown more and more stereotypical. I greet my husband at the door with cheese dip. I watch him take off his suit and hear about his day. We watch *Jeopardy!* and I win. We have supper. He goes to clean up the kitchen and I wave off his help. Write what I know, who wants to read that? If only our apartment was haunted or I was the tiniest bit possessed by the devil.

———

The next morning, there is a school bus waiting to take us to our new challenge, the Annual Tivoli Yard Sale. After cameramen take their seats for a loading shot, Mitzy and I are the first contestants to board. As winners of the last challenge, we have our choice of seats. I look to Mitzy to decide. She's closer in age to public high school than I am, and probably sat in the most popular spot.

But Mitzy isn't moving past the rubber threshold of the accordion door. The smell of pleather seats, slit and juiced with ninth-grade-boy Red Man dip spit is transporting her back in time to when she was not the centerfold of attention. And now I remember: cheerleaders don't become *Playboy* bunnies. Knock-kneed, brace-faced, flat-chested, brunette band geeks become bunnies because they want everyone to know that after hocking their trombones for rhinoplasty, they are just as beautiful as the girl who dates the quarterback.

F'in Tiny is in the front seat usually reserved for teachers, chaperones, and mentally handicapped kids. He says, "Mitzy, one foot in front of the other. Chop, chop! Maybe if you swallow your gum, you can walk."

Oh man, she swallows it.

Behind me, the Scientologists are getting restless, and I feel a twenty-million-dollar-a-movie hand on my back. I coax Mitzy up the bus stairs and into the belly of the sense-memory beast. She stumbles forward, glancing over her shoulder for approval. I nod for her to sit three rows back, but don't follow her.

I realize that I am at an age where I don't care about who I sit by or what the person I don't sit by thinks of me or what anybody else thinks of me either. I am the author of three unpublished novels. Failure. Failure. And one to grow on. My worst nightmare has repeated itself every few years. And you know what? Life goes on with or without your book in print. Life will go on if I don't sit by Mitzy. I am genuinely fond of her, but for this challenge we are Dumpster diving on our own. I need every advantage I can get. I want to be the first one off this bus. I want to win.

I plop down next to F'in Tiny, who pops up when my weight hits the cushion. He pops up so high that his head goes out of frame and a producer makes us reenact the moment. Oh. Great. I do care what people think. I feel terrible as I snub Mitzy in slow motion this time. I ease down next to F'in Tiny, who's braced himself as if I am a high-dive donkey and his seat is a kiddie pool.

Everyone else piles onto the bus and streams past Mitzy, who studiously presses at her replacement press-on nails. I'm relieved when John Lithgow asks if he can sit next to her. As the bus pulls onto the road, I expect he'll soon have us singing rounds of "She'll Be Coming 'Round the Mountain When She Comes!"

Directly behind me are the Scientologists. The wife taps my shoulder. She says, "Nice move, girl. Good seat. You got gump."

"Gump?" I ask.

"Yeah, girl, gump. *Gumption.* We've been watching you. We're impressed."

By "we" the Scientologist wife means her and her husband. I've seen them interviewed on TV and they always refer to themselves as a unit. *She* didn't support Hillary Clinton, *they* did. *He* didn't choose to make the move from comedies to action/drama and biopics, *they* did. *They* chose to have twins through fertility treatments, and then *they* chose to battle her postpartum depression without drugs or psychotherapy. *They* chose to send her off to a yurt for two months. When she came home, *they* got her a supporting role in a movie in which she bared her stretch marks under overhead lighting. The part earned her a Golden Globe nomination. And then *they* decided that she would stay at home with the kids. For the last fifteen years, she hasn't done more than cameos in his blockbusters. So, I'm guessing—now that the twins are practically grown—she's done her time and *they* are here for *her* comeback.

I ask, "Which one of you is the collector?"

The actor opens his mouth, but his wife puts her hand on his arm. She stops him. From saying what? Another *we*? What's wrong with *we*? *We* is their thing. Aren't they on *Dumpster Diving with the Stars* to get *we* a TV series starring *we* as a mortician with great arms in a man's world?

She tells him, "Take it easy, baby."

He chuckles what I'm guessing is his marriage chuckle. All we marrieds have a marriage chuckle. A marriage chuckle is a fake laugh you bring out when your spouse does something dumb that you have to pretend is charming. My marriage chuckle is for when my husband tells our new friends that he doesn't believe in brunch. The Scientologist husband's must be for when his wife preempts his dumb thing.

Speaking of dumb things, F'in Tiny has perked up. He's on his knees, arms draped over the back of our seat, leaning deep into the Scientologists' personal space. He asks the wife, "Are you concerned that if your husband exposes his love for antiquing, his fans will no longer see him as a leading man?"

Camera lights burn down upon us. Only one cameraman has stayed at the back of the bus to film Verbena, who is hanging her head out a window, flying her freak flag of long brown hair, and pumping her arm to get semi-truck drivers to honk their horns. John Lithgow looks like he's giving good fatherly advice to Mitzy (this could be the moment when she decides to go to community college), but the producers don't care. F'in Tiny is off his iPhone and onto something. And, by God, they will capture it.

Cardinal Reality Rule #3: Strain relationships. Ask uncomfortable questions. Put one member in physical danger. Split 'em. Viewers like to see other couples more miserable than themselves.

The Scientologist wife knows this, and she is not having it. She says, "Weren't you an actor once, Elvin? You love antiquing. *You're on the show.*"

"I'm the host."

"There's a difference?"

F'in Tiny says, "Antiquing is one thing, parading a wife around to stay number one at the box office is quite another."

The Scientologist wife says, "The secret to why our marriage works is that everybody helps everybody. We're a team. At home and on this show."

"But this isn't a team show," says F'in Tiny.

He's right. This is not *The Amazing Race.* For the rest of filming, the Scientologists will have to compete against each other. It's not something I would ever do with my husband, but if there's one thing I've learned in life it's that people do things I don't.

F'in Tiny prods. "Teamwork. Really? *Teamwork* is your big secret?"

I know what F'in Tiny is inferring because whenever

he is interviewed reporters infer the same thing about him. They ask about his string of chiseled male personal trainers. They say, "Because you were a fat kid. Really? Because you were *a fat kid* is why you are so body conscious now?"

The Scientologist actor looks to his wife for an answer.

She is stoic. She maintains eye contact with F'in Tiny. She doesn't blink. Her stare dares him to ask his inane question again. On TV, this will read as confident, but up close I can see that she is frozen because she is scared.

I say, "The secret to our marriage is separate bathrooms."

The Scientologists laugh, real laughter because they've both been holding their breath. F'in Tiny cuts me a look. I've broken his spell. He turns and slumps in his seat. He pulls out his iPhone and thumb-flicks the screen. The cameramen know all is lost and retreat.

As I face forward, I get a twenty-million-dollar squeeze on the shoulder.

———

When our bus rolls into a church parking lot in Tivoli, New York, a cameraman slips out the emergency exit and comes around to the front of the bus to set up a shot of our mass exodus. Through the windows, about a quarter mile in the distance, I see that residents have chalked off squares of pavement along Main Street and piled card tables high with boxes and trunks hauled down from their attics. I reapply my lipstick, snap my purse shut, and smooth my starched skirt. This is supposed to be a less down-and-dirty event.

F'in Tiny climbs over me with a tight straddle to reach the aisle. The engine idles as he dons a new hat for this segment. The Indiana Jones fedora is too large, and the brim tips over one eye without any assistance. He holds his whip like a jump rope.

He says, "For this challenge you will have FIFTY minutes and FIFTY dollars to scour this small AMERICAN YARD SALE. The WINNER's find will have the BIGGEST difference between what you pay for it and market value. And, as always on *Dumpster Diving with the Stars,* you do not have to spend anything. The MORE you save, the MORE your find will be worth. Currently, THE *PLAYBOY* BUNNY and THE WRITER are tied for the lead. ARE. YOU. READY? Dumpster divers?"

Now we know what to do.

Mario drums his Crocs on the floor and we shout, "Yes!"

John Lithgow shouts, "Tally-ho!" He's got his arm around Mitzy's shoulders and gives her a squeeze. He's rooting for her. He's rooting for all of us.

If only I'd sat by Mitzy, maybe I too would feel his arm around my shoulders. But I sat in the front because I wanted a head start.

"On your mark." F'in Tiny raises a stopwatch. "Get set."

The bus driver cranks open the accordion door. The bus rocks with our eagerness. Contestants rock in their seats.

To add to our anxiety, F'in Tiny stands firm, blocking the aisle. He takes a deliberately long breath. Holds it. Then stage-whispers, "Go!"

Contestants and cameramen surge forward.

F'in Tiny hops out of their way, but back into *my* seat blocking only *my* escape. He smirks. He'll teach me not to butt into his interview.

I vault over the seat barrier.

The Scientologist shrieks like one of his fans when I drop down in front of him, cutting him off at the door.

Ha HA! I'm the first one on land.

The dew smells good. I am running, running, running! But I slip. I fall flat-out, grass-burning my knees and the undersides of my wrists. I recover! I'm on my feet, charging the sale, maintaining my lead, clutching my purse like a football, fueled by the humiliation that when I fell my skirt flipped over my head revealing what the cameras will not lie about: beige cotton underpants with a waistband as thick and wide as a ruler.

The Scientologist and his wife easily overtake me, but Berkshire Theatre fans slow Lithgow, and the tennis player gets her heels stuck in the lawn. Mario and Verbena chug ahead and blend into the crowd. When I finish eating Mitzy's dust, I catch up to find her lingering at the entrance to Main Street. She is stalled at the mouth of the yard sale just like she was when she was boarding the bus.

It's the smell and sight of books that have her in their clutches this time. Books are everywhere: hardbacks, paperbacks, mass market, trade; books with leather binding, embossed gold-leaf titles; it's a maze of spines. The bookshelves that the books are sitting on are for sale. One card table has a heap of paper grocery sacks with a sign that reads: "Pack a bag for a buck!"

Mitzy says, "Bitzy's the reader."

I nudge her forward into the thicket of yard sellers. For every yard seller, there are forty shoppers. While there are plenty of knickknacks (ashtrays, marble fruit, Grecian lady lamps), they are buffered by books. It's hard to know where to dive in. Once again, Mitzy has clamped on to my hand. I wriggle free to point out an antique car and bike area at the far end of the market. Surely she knows from auto shows. I lock my eyes on a row of overpriced Nancy Drews. I try to get my gump up to barter, but Mitzy's still a shadow.

She says, "Bitzy took three books to the hospital for her recovery. They're supposed to be funny, but I don't feel her laughing. When she laughs, I get the hiccups."

F'in Tiny says, "Wouldn't we all like to see that!"

I swear he must have tunneled here.

Mitzy asks him, "Have you heard from Hef? Is Bitzy okay?"

F'in Tiny brandishes his stopwatch. "The show, honey. The show."

Mitzy shouldn't be asking about her sister on camera. F'in Tiny is not going to answer her. Unless World War III breaks out and Bitzy's been elected commander in chief, Mitzy and the rest of us signed contracts to Dumpster dive in the dark. She's slowing our segment.

F'in Tiny says, "You're working, honey. Get to work."

From deep within the yard sale comes the fan-like shriek of the Scientologist.

F'in Tiny jerks in its direction. He tamps his hat on his head and elbows through browsers. Mitzy drags me along. It's a middle-aged mosh pit. But then a camera-man gets in front of us, and folks clear a path as if he's an ambulance.

The Scientologist is trying to contain himself. The booth he's in borders the auto area and is run by a gentleman with a braided beard who sells spare parts. The man's wife sits on a stool by a cashbox, where she'd been reading until the Scientologist asked to buy the book out of her hands.

The book is an Amy Madeline.

"Come on," says the Scientologist. "You're not even

ten pages in. I'll double your money. How much did you pay for it?"

The woman says, "Fifty cents." She closes the book, saving her place with a finger. She studies the glossy rose-colored cover. She asks, "What's it to you?"

F'in Tiny says, "Yes, tell us all. What *is* it to you?"

I know what it is.

It's a rare first edition with a typo the size of Texas. A copy editor got fired over that typo. A hundred thousand copies were pulped because of that typo. Riding the surprise hit of Amy Madeline's first novel, her rose-colored second novel was rushed to print. Her main character was a pastry chef, and an autocorrected joke wasn't reversed, so that every time the nice lady stuffed her face with *cake,* she ate *cock.* Reprints were published with a lilac cover. Finding a rose-colored cover is as hard as finding a real-life sixty-hour-a-week pastry chef who'll perform fellatio with the frequency and gusto that Amy Madeline's character did.

The Scientologist wife tells the lady, "He's just joking with you, girl."

Disappointment flashes across the Scientologist's face, but he masks it with a marriage chuckle. He must be a closeted fan of Amy Madeline's: a Mad Hag. Only Mad Hags know about this particular book. I wonder if he knows that this book is dedicated to me. I wonder if the producers know. I wonder if they planted it for me to find. Judging by their interest in the auto area, where Mitzy is riding a rusty tricycle like a sexy toddler, they didn't.

I am as invisible as I am at Amy Madeline's readings, where I sit in the front row, holding her purse. In literary circles, I'm not known as Amy Madeline's peer anymore. I'm her wing woman. As a Mad Hag, I'd think the Scientologist would know about her campaign to get me on the show, but he hasn't mentioned it. Nobody else on this show had mentioned it either. To *Dumpster Diving with the Stars,* I'm just *the writer.* I could be any writer. I could be Amy Madeline. They don't know *Portnoy's Complaint* from *Pet Sematary.* *Cardinal Reality Rule #4: Appeal to a new audience.* I'm a novelty—like a disabled vet or a little person—cast as a new way to breathe new life into an old show.

I say, "I'll buy it." And I whip out my fifty.

The biker's wife snaps up her quick hundred percent profit and hands me the book, which turns out to be worth six hundred dollars more than I paid.

Mitzy's trike is worth seventy-five. John Lithgow suffers a thirty-five-dollar forgery penalty because Herman Melville never signed a book with a ballpoint. Mario Batali's music box is worth a hundred. The tennis player breaks even with her "folk art" (three stuffed animals sewn together like a totem pole). Verbena comes in a close second to me with a cigar box full of Rat Pack–era casino matchbooks. The Scientologist wife comes in third with a musket.

She pouts about her loss but throws a tantrum about her husband's low score. She demands that the local appraisers get a second opinion on his Harley Davidson bicycle crank. "I mean," she says directly to the camera, "it's a Harley. *We* know it's got to be worth more than that."

The Scientologist says, "Baby, let it go. Enjoy your own score. We're cool."

"We are?"

He says to the camera, "Hey, all we can do is buy what we like."

What they've bought is extra camera time to show the world that the Scientologist millionaire movie star is just a "regular guy." Just like a regular guy, he passed up six-hundred-dollar chick lit in favor of something he can slather in grease. But I know he's a Mad Hag. And I know that he knew the value of the rose-colored book. So I figure, he threw this challenge. As he is going to throw every future challenge to look like a regular guy. No wonder his wife's face doesn't have a line on it. It's not Botox that's kept her young looking, it's lying.

The Scientologists aren't here to revive her career. *They* are here to disprove gay rumors about *him*. So, why would he come on a show that promotes the most stereo-typically gay pastime? Easy. It's like me writing a novel called *How I Murdered My Husband and Got Away with It* and then murdering my husband.

———

As a reality game show fan, I understand that I'm manipu-lated to root for certain contestants. *Cardinal Reality Rule #5: Play favorites.* Producers make nice people look nice and not-so-nice people look evil. You think you don't have a foul mouth? Well, here's a reel of the twenty-three times you called your wife a bleeping slowpoke. When my season of *Dumpster Diving with the Stars* airs, I'm guessing that the Scientologist will be cast as the handsome dope, his wife as the smother mother, Verbena as the hillbilly, Mario and Lithgow as good sports (aka themselves), and the tennis player as the bitch.

The tennis player is a lovely woman, but our entire cast is lovely, so our producers are scrambling. In my interviews they've asked me what I think about the ten-nis player's four suitcases, one of which is entirely filled with red-soled Christian Louboutins. They've asked me to compare her loud voice to some type of machinery that is equally loud. When I answer that her shoes are her business and her tone of voice is fine by me, the produc-ers are annoyed.

"We thought you were supposed to be the writer."

"I *am* a writer." My voice cracks.

Damn. I know this will be the audio clip they play over my ravine-water-stained face or big beige panties reveal every week in the opening credits.

I say, "There's more to life than writing." And wish they'd pick that audio clip. But they won't. I feign traveler's diarrhea and excuse myself from the interview before I start to weep and am cast as the premenopausal washed-up emotional wreck.

The thing is, we've got one more challenge (our tenth) to go and I'm winning—by a lot.

On our third challenge, when F'in Tiny sent us to treasure hunt in Tori Spelling's convoy of moving vans (to coincide with the start of her new reality show in which she and her husband try to get their kids into private school in Manhattan), I picked the oil painting of her mother Candy in a Halston dress because I knew the frame probably once held a Renoir. On our fourth challenge, when we spent the night in a colonial house, I bagged the porcelain doll that wouldn't stop staring at Mario. Sure, I lost later challenges to Verbena's thousand-dollar bill that she fished out of a cuckoo clock, and John Lithgow's Confederate sword, and we were all shocked that the Scientologist's motorized Barcalounger was worth fourteen hundred, but my profits have put me way out in front.

The producers aren't happy about it.

Looks like, unless we're raging drunkards, writers are boring. Who's going to root for me, a woman who, in her downtime, reads fat Russian tomes under the low lights of B&B sitting rooms?

Mitzy, a much more desirable champion for the show (little girl lost turns family-friendly decorator, and think of all those tank-topped running shots), had an equal chance of maintaining our original rocking horse lead, but her enthusiasm has waned. She's left a trail of press-on nails along the Atlantic seaboard. She is the youngest among us, but she lags behind. She stoops. She's put on weight. She has night terrors about contracting Legionnaires' disease in the Playboy Mansion grotto.

She tells me, "It happened to Bitzy. She says you feel like you're a hairless dog in a mohair sweater trapped in a car."

I say, "That's so specific."

Mitzy says, "My sister's smart like that."

I say, "I'm sure she's okay."

But I'm not.

Producers still haven't told Mitzy how Bitzy's surgery went.

If it were my husband who might be lying somewhere comatose from anesthesia complications, I'd have quit this show a month ago and risked a lawsuit to find out. But I'm a grown-ass lady with savings, mutual funds, and property in my name. All Mitzy has is a room and her looks.

For our final challenge, which takes place at the Pennsylvania estate auction of Mrs. Giles Everett Preston III, F'in Tiny saunters into the dead woman's crowded ballroom wearing a smoking jacket and an ascot. He (or the costume department) is under the impression that old money dresses like Professor Plum. He holds his pipe to his face like a monocle.

Over the din of hundreds of antique dealers, interior designers, mom bloggers, and looky-loos, F'in Tiny says, "For this challenge you will have FOUR hours and FOUR HUNDRED dollars to bid during this small AMERICAN ESTATE AUCTION. The WINNER's find will have the BIGGEST difference between what you pay for it and market value. Currently, THE WRITER has the lead. But an estate auction like this is full of surprises. Any one of you could pull ahead and win. Even you, Mitzy. Mitzy! Hello?"

Mitzy is huddled in a back-row auction chair. She cups her stomach as if her belly button might pop out like a turkey timer. The girl is sick with worry about her sister.

We contestants are sick with worry about Mitzy. We sit in front and to the sides of her protectively. If there is such a thing as twin sensory perception, it is radiating off Mitzy like a third-degree burn.

"ARE. YOU. READY? Dumpster divers?"

We are not ready.

"I SAID—"

From the front of the ballroom, which is packed to the stained-glass Tiffany windows (each available at starting bids of $150,000), the auctioneer taps his gavel. He directs his gaze at F'in Tiny. *Dumpster Diving with the Stars* is a guest in Mrs. Giles Everett Preston III's palatial country home. The auctioneer is the gentleman with his name in the catalog, which means that he is the host, not F'in Tiny. With his tap, the auctioneer is giving F'in Tiny and his band of interlopers one and only one do-over to get what will surely be our bridled fervor on tape.

F'in Tiny clears his throat and slips his pipe in his pocket. He ignores a boom microphone that a producer has ordered to be dangled above his blond highlights. He asks, "Are you ready, Dumpster divers?"

We nod like a secretary's desk edge of bobbleheads. Out of respect to Mrs. Giles Everett Preston III and for Mitzy's sake, we are not going to whoop it up.

The auction begins.

Verbena is the first Dumpster diver to raise her paddle. She thrusts it up like the Day-Glo flag she waves to signal worm pits in the woods on *Nightcrawlers.* She wants Mrs. Giles Everett Preston III's mismatched sugar bowl, and I think she may go so far as to stand on her chair and jockey across the heads of other bidders to get it.

The auctioneer says, "Do I have a hundred? One-twenty-five? One-fifty? Two?"

He most certainly does. And how. The sugar bowl is snatched from Verbena's grasp and sells for three thousand, two hundred and twenty-five bucks.

Turns out, the sugar bowl has a story behind it. As the auctioneer drove up the price, he revealed that the reason it is mismatched is because it is the only piece from its set that Mrs. Giles Everett Preston III did not hurl at her husband when she found him under the dining room table "clotting the cream" of the then Earl of Sandwich.

As the auction continues, we discover that everything has a story. Lithgow is outbid for a Cole Porter Playbill because Cole Porter composed one of the musical's numbers on Mrs. Giles Everett Preston III's grand piano, and while he composed it she pretended not to hear her husband cry out from a maid's room for his epilepsy pills. Mario loses a ceramic soup tureen shaped like a pumpkin because Mrs. Giles Everett Preston III used it to mask the lime green hue of the vichyssoise she poisoned when her husband gave her HPV for Thanksgiving. Suffocating needlepoint pillows, bludgeoning candelabras, and a fountain pen used to fake a suicide note are all lost (along with three-fourths of the lots) because bidders with more money to bid with than us want to own something that belonged to an eccentric.

F'in Tiny demands the producers give us bigger

allowances. He says, "I'll dub over the intro in post. You know: 'UNLIMITED TIME and FOUR THOUSAND dollars.' Give it to them."

The producers agree.

Four grand opens up more of the small remainder of the catalog. We flip through the back quarter-inch of stiff high-quality gloss pages we hadn't dog-eared. We sneak peeks at what other contestants are pausing to look at. The auctioneer never stops auctioning. The rest of the audience never stops raising their paddles. We are awash in the anxiety of new possibilities. But these possibilities grow fewer and farther between and with every passing moment they are going, going, gone!

We squirm in our seats. F'in Tiny paces behind us. A potbellied cameraman tries to keep up with him. Other cameramen circle the room. Producers grip and gripe into iPhones. Their finale is more frenzied than they'd expected. Only Mitzy is as motionless as she's been since the start.

I slide my catalog onto her lap. I flip and lift photos of jewelry. See? Here's a ladybug ring that can hold a teaspoon of cyanide. See? Here's a charm bracelet of lab test subjects, or as the lady of the house called them, her babies (gigantic cats). It kills me that Mitzy doesn't respond. There are so many things that should make her say, "Cooooot!"

F'in Tiny leans over her and lifts her paddle from her lap. He says, "Your arms don't work, Mitzy? There's nothing you want of Mrs. the Third's?"

John Lithgow says, "Let the poor girl alone. So what if she doesn't bid?"

F'in Tiny says, "This is a game, John. Mitzy signed a contract for the love of the thrift. She needs to participate. She needs to be *active*. The game's almost over. She plays, and *then* she gets to go home."

John Lithgow says, "And what exactly will she find when she gets home, sir? Will she find everything as she left it?"

"Her room at the mansion is waiting for her."

"And will *everyone* be there waiting for her?"

"What do you think, John? It's a twenty-room mansion with a hundred birds on the property."

I say, "Birds aren't family."

"That's right," says John Lithgow. "What's important is *family*."

F'in Tiny says, "Mitzy's *family* needs her to win."

A teardrop appears in the corner of Mitzy's eye, and that teardrop is shinier than any sequin she's ever affixed to her body.

F'in Tiny offers her a handkerchief, pulled out of his pocket like a magician's bottomless supply.

Mitzy won't take it. She doesn't want anything more to

do with him or this show. She shakes her head and her teardrop plummets.

F'in Tiny presses in. The velvet knot of his smoking jacket rubs against the back of her head.

I cringe because I can feel his fingers sinking into her shoulders. I want his hands off of her. And so my hand, gripping my paddle, shoots up and sideswipes his ear.

The auctioneer says, "One thousand dollars from the lady in the cardigan!"

I have no idea what I'm bidding for, but it must be good because F'in Tiny ignores the blood pulsing out of his ear.

He says, "Mitzy, you're going to let her get away with it? The *writer*?" He says the word with such venom that he draws everyone's attention.

I say, "I'm a Dumpster diver. And I'm on to you. You only want Mitzy to win so Bitzy's surgery will sell your show. If Mitzy wins, people will watch *until* she wins because they'll want to see her poor, sweet face when she finds out what you've been keeping from her because whatever it is, it must be god-awful. *Cardinal Reality Rule #6: Tug heartstrings.* The best person to root for is a contestant with a sob story."

F'in Tiny says, "*Cardinal reality rule?* What are you talking about? Why are you talking *like that*?"

Oh, look what I found. I say, "I'm writing."

"Well, do it on your own time. This is TV."

Mitzy asks, "Is it true what she said? Is Bitzy bad off?"

F'in Tiny says, "I can assure you that your sister is in the very best hands."

John Lithgow says, "Shameful."

The tennis player says, "That's messed up."

It is, but it doesn't stop me from foreseeing that when the opening credits roll each week, the tennis player's audio clip will be run over a loop of Mario Batali eating a corn dog.

Verbena frowns. We all know *Nightcrawlers* would never pull something as manipulative as this.

"One-thousand-one-hundred, ladies and gentle-men?" The auctioneer is going on with his show. "Do I have one-thousand-one-hundred for this lovely fish-plate by Lewis Straus and Sons?"

He does not. Wait, fishplate?

"One-thousand-one-hundred? It has a lovely painting of a fish on it."

That's the best story he can come up with?

F'in Tiny says, "Mitzy, bid, I beg of you. None of you have won anything of this crazy old bag's. The auction's almost over. If the writer wins the plate, she'll win the whole show. We can't have that. Nobody knows who she is. She's never been in *Playboy*. She's never been in— what's *Playboy* for writers?"

Mario Batali says, *"The New Yorker."*

"Does she show her tits in *The New Yorker*?"

The auctioneer holds his gavel extra high for the cameras. "One-thousand-one-hundred going once."

F'in Tiny shouts, "Come on!" He's on his tiny feet in tiny shoes with tiny lifts, wriggling his way between two un-tiny cameramen. He charges the auctioneer, who won't give up his gavel despite the fight he's being given.

"Going twice."

F'in Tiny shouts, "I *knew* bringing a writer on was a mistake! She's like those Telenovela Mexicans they keep bringing on *Dancing with the Stars*—but without the abs. This writer has no abs! Mitzy! Somebody! Anybody! One of you Dumpster divers bid!"

No one bids. John Lithgow holds Mitzy, who sobs into his chest. Mario Batali and the tennis player cross their arms in disgust. Verbena tilts her head down so that her hair shields her face. In solidarity with Mitzy, the other contestants will concede, let me win, and punish F'in Tiny and his f'in tiny show.

F'in Tiny screams at the Scientologist, "Bid, dammit! Here's your chance! You win this and you win the unconditional love of every red-blooded AMERICAN HOUSEWIFE!"

Always camera ready, the Scientologist says, "Sorry, Smalls, no can do. I have my sights set on that secretarial desk."

His wife chuckles.

"Wait, that's not right?"

She says, "It's fine, baby."

And it is fine. It's all going to work out fine. The Scientologists' marriage, the tennis player's rep, Verbena's return to hill country, Batali's and Lithgow's continued success, Mitzy's life after *Playboy,* and my new novel that will begin: *Cardinal Reality Rule #7: Forge unlikely friendships.*

I keep my paddle raised until I hear "Sold."

SOUTHERN LADY CODE

I s this too dressy?" is Southern Lady code for: I look fabulous and it would be in your best interest to tell me so.

"I'm not crazy about it" is code for: I hate that more than sugar-free punch.

"What do you think about her?" is code for: I don't like her.

"She's always been lovely to me" is code for: I don't like her either.

"She has a big personality" means she's loud as a T. rex.

"She's the nicest person" means she's boring as pound cake.

"She has beautiful skin" means she's white as a tampon.

"She's old" means she's racist as Sandy Duncan in *Roots.*

"You are so bad!" is Southern Lady code for: That is the tackiest thing I've ever heard and I am delighted that you shared it with me.

"No, you're so bad!" is code for: Let's snitch and bitch.

"She's a character" means drunk.

"She has a good time" means slut.

"She's sweet" means Asperger's.

"She's outdoorsy" means lesbian.

"Hmm" is Southern Lady code for: I don't agree with you but am polite enough not to rub your nose in your ignorance.

"Nice talking with you" is code for: Party's over, now scoot.

HELLO!

WELCOME TO BOOK CLUB

H ello! Welcome to Book Club. I'm your hostess. My Book Club name is Mary Beth. We all have Book Club names at Book Club.

Why, dear? Well, really, why not?

The girl who brought you here goes by Delores. The ladies on the red sofa named themselves after TV judges. The ladies on the gray sofa named themselves after the Supremes. The ladies at the buffet table chose Bethany, Marjorie, and Aretha. The elderly lady dozing off in the egg chair calls herself Jane.

If you decide to join us, you can give yourself a Book Club name. We'll laminate a bookmark with your new name on it. We'll hole-punch a tassel. You can keep your bookmark in whatever book you're reading. It doesn't have to be a Book Club book. But your Book Club name will be a secret name that only we call you. Trust me, you'll like it. It feels like a dollar bill in your bra.

That's right, Jane, I'm talking about bras at Book Club again! Look who's awake!

Jane's our grande dame. She's ninety years young. She's what you call a "real New Yorker." Meaning: she's loaded. When it comes to Jane's money, think of a crazy amount of money, *lottery money* that you'd like as a windfall. Imagine hundred-dollar bills funneling around you like a tornado of financial freedom. Now double that money. Honestly, triple it. Then add a billion.

It sounds better than handing out towels at Flywheel, doesn't it, dear?

Yes, I bet it does.

I met Jane at a library lecture by Stephen King. Can you believe this sweet-looking lady who has Chanel suits like some girls have days-of-the-week underpants loves horror novels? She sure does. And that means, from time to time, Book Club loves them too. Personally, I think her love of blood and guts and things that go mwah-ha-ha in the night has to do with her want to invest time and money into things more horrible than what's happened to her in real life. Jane's survived two husbands (one had a stroke, and one's mistress shot him dead in a sex swing) and three children (car accident, ski accident, and one "fell" off the roof of her house).

My dear, please don't concern yourself, Jane's fine. They all died years ago. And here's what nobody tells you: losing a child isn't the end of the world. Life goes on—and more often than not, goes on quite nicely. Just look at Jane with her feet up on my coffee table. Have you ever seen a woman look more relaxed?

Delores, would you refill Jane's Scotch and soda, please and thank you!

See there: look at Delores scurry away from the cheese plate. At Book Club, Jane's waited on hand and foot because Jane is Book Club's patron of the arts. Jane buys everyone's Book Club book in hardback, and tickets for us to attend literary events. If you join Book Club, Jane will take on your Book Club expenses too. All you have to do is pick your preferred theater seating.

The ladies on the red sofa like to sit center orchestra for the acoustics. The ladies on the gray sofa migrate to mezzanines so they can whisper. The ladies at the buffet table are claustrophobic, so they ride an aisle like a bobsled. Delores never stops texting, so she sits at the back. It takes a certain kind of woman to sit in the front. Jane and I are that kind of woman: a front-row woman.

A front-row woman is a participant. She never breaks eye contact with the speaker. She laughs when he says something funny, and she makes a funny face when he describes something gross. That day in the front row of Stephen King, Jane and I had so many facial tics the librarians must have thought that strokes were contagious.

How many strokes have you had, Jane?

That many! My God, it's going to take a bolt of lightning to take you out.

Two bolts and a frying pan to the back of the head? Oh, Jane, you kill me.

She still can't smile right.

I know it's not your fault, Bethany! I didn't say it was your fault!

Bethany is the woman at the buffet table without a plate, to the right of the Caesar salad, rearranging my napkins. She's Jane's neurologist. She joined Book Club because Jane invited her to join. She's forty-something like the rest of us—except for Delores, who's just out of college—and should have known better than to choose a Book Club name so close to mine. Bethany, Mary *Beth*. Honestly, the nerve. But tolerating such indiscretions makes me a good hostess.

A good hostess is gracious and doesn't make a big deal about things like a guest showing up in the same Tory Burch tunic. But a same-tunic disaster is only going to happen once in a blue moon, especially now that I will call you a week before Book Club to make note of your outfit. Book Club names are forever.

Yes, I know you can hear me, Bethany! Would you like to take my husband's last name as well? Just kidding!

Bethany works sixteen-hour days and is on call all the time and thus has never married. She wants a baby and for whatever reason wants to personally give birth to that baby, and she refuses to have one-night stands or steal hospital sperm samples, so her biological clock is deafening.

Not like yours, dear. At your age, your fertility is like a pocket watch swaddled in cotton, drawn up in a velvet pouch and tucked inside a Pringles can.

But Bethany's! Sometimes I walk past the Fifth Avenue Synagogue and am frightened a bomb is about to go off. I imagine my upper torso landing in a gyro cart and the contents of my purse laid out for all to see. Then, I realize it's not anxiety hounding me; it's Bethany's biological clock. It ticks so loud, I'm amazed Mount Sinai isn't evacuated on a daily basis.

Oh, Bethany, don't make that face! You know it's true!

Bethany likes Book Club to read romances and I am talking straight-to-mass-market-paperback Harlequin romance romances. She likes her heroines overpowered.

These days, we'd call what Bethany likes Book Club to read "rape." But in Bethany's bodice-rippers, throwing twelve layers of underskirts up over a heroine's face and plowing her like a cotton field is known as the main character getting her "just deserts." Honestly, it's like rape is no worse than having a banana cream pie shoved in your face. At first you're startled, probably hurt, but then you get a taste of your assaulter's meringue and realize you want to eat it every damned day.

Book Club is potluck. The ladies on the red sofa don't eat curry. The ladies on the gray sofa don't eat shellfish. I hate shredded coconut. Jane's diabetic, but will eat anything she darned well pleases.

Won't you, Jane?

Yes ma'am, open-heart surgery, your foot!

Then there's Bethany, who is lactose intolerant, gluten intolerant, vegan, and has irritable bowel syndrome, which is all code for anorexic. She's a garnish girl. So, throw a radish rose on the edge of whatever you bring and she'll feast on that. Honestly, watch her tonight. She'll suck that celery stick like a Whistle Pop.

I am always in charge of the menu. So I'll call you before our next meeting and help you decide what to bring. I have a chart. So, for example, next to my name this month it says: Tory Burch hedgehog tunic and bacon-wrapped water chestnuts.

No, it's not a spreadsheet. It's something more akin to our mothers' PTA phone trees. You're too young to remember phone trees.

Oh, you've heard of them? Well, aren't you an elephant-never-forgets.

Not elephant as in fat, dear—I'll bet you've never been on a diet. You can probably have as many bacon-wrapped water chestnuts as you want and never gain weight. What I meant was elephant as being good at remembering. Come to think of it, dear, along with a lack of fat cells, were you blessed with a lack of Alzheimer's in your family history?

You were! How nice. And how old are you exactly, twenty-seven?

Twenty-six. Even better. Not like Delores over there with her arm elbow deep in the onion dip. She's twenty-two and would guess a phone tree is something Matthew Barney glued together for MOMA.

Oh hush, Delores, you know you don't know what a phone tree is! You don't know the landline number to this apartment. Don't you dare scroll, Delores. Use your mem-or-ree. It's in your head, where you keep your will to live.

Honestly, I swear, I let that girl into Book Club as a favor to her dear departed mother—who along with me was a founding member of Book Club—and I regret it every month. Delores always nominates books that are the first in a trilogy.

Delores's Book Club choices are YA. YA stands for young adult. Young adult is meant for teenagers the way *Seventeen* is meant for twelve-year-olds, meaning Delores is too old for it, but she and her Smith sisters cannot get enough. YA is about angst. Will I get that boy to like me? Will I lose the weight? Will I turn into a vampire if he just gives me a hickey? I'm an orphan! I'm a mind reader! I'm biracial! I'm gay! When I get out of high school, I'll move to New York City, where I'll find others like me, and then I'll be happy and I will have it all: a career, a family, good teeth, and takeout Chinese.

Delores has a twisted uterus, is unemployed, and lives in my guest room. She has a fashion blog, which means she posts Instagrams on her Tumblr page of what she wears every day. She used to have a book blog, but gave it up because joining Book Club shuts that sort of public opinionating down.

But you can talk about your feelings here, isn't that right, Delores?

Yes, you have so very many feelings.

What Delores frets over on a regular basis, dear, is that having "it all" is harder than she thought it would be. At every Book Club, the rest of us old marrieds try to save Delores years of aggravation by explaining to her that she cannot have it all. It all is overrated.

Am I right, ladies?

Nodding, nodding, nodding. It's like we're listening to rap!

Except for Bethany, over there. She refuses to be swayed. Bethany's an overachiever and doesn't understand why she can't rope a man into marrying and impregnating her.

Because men aren't bulls and the Upper East Side is not a rodeo, Bethany!

Marriage wasn't the best choice for you, was it, dear? You're divorced, am I correct?

Yes, and your ex-husband left you with a mountain of debt because his idea of having it all was maxing out your joint credit cards on Internet poker. I'm sure everyone's already said to you: Thank God you don't have children. Well, there's a reason for that. Children cost money and a great deal of your attention. Every night, I tell Delores before she turns in for bed that she should thank her lucky stars for her twisted uterus. It's one less choice she has to make.

Well, it is, Delores! Not everyone's meant to experience childbirth.

Except for you, my dear. You look positively born for it. You'll bounce back from your divorce. And you know what helps?

That's right! Book Club.

Oh Delores, buck up. Grab a tissue from Jane's sweater sleeve. And I implore you, take Marjorie up on her offer of that paying job at Talbots.

Marjorie is the lady with a thermometer in her mouth. You thought it was a swizzle stick, dear?

Honestly, so did I years ago when I brought my catalog returns into the Seventy-Second Street Talbots. Marjorie is the manager and was working the register.

Just look at her, she is the epitome of taste: so much plaid and cashmere; and only one piece of jewelry in addition to her wedding set. She has a stunning brooch collection. It rivals Madeleine Albright's. She's wearing my favorite brooch today: a ceramic bunny with tiny onyx eyes.

That's right, dear, we're all wearing that brooch. You're very observant. What an excellent quality to have in your gene pool.

And guess what: as a member of Book Club, you'll get Marjorie's 40 percent employee discount. That goes for sale items too. Can you believe it?

I know!

Lucky for us, pleats are back. Lucky for Marjorie, her health benefits are stellar. Talbots has paid for Marjorie and her husband to have in vitro six times. They have zero children. But there are pickling jars in their pantry that we don't discuss.

I'm not discussing them, Marjorie!

Marjorie loves celebrity memoirs. She likes to have Book Club read about beautiful people who remain beautiful people despite life's little challenges such as bankruptcy, infidelity, alcoholism, and infertility.

You've had three out of four of these challenges, haven't you, dear?

Yes, that worthless cheating drunk of an ex-husband of yours left you feeling lower than dirt. But, let me assure you, you are a treasure. And Book Club is going to dig you out!

Men. Famous men are the worst. Did you know Frank Langella had an affair with Dinah Shore? He seduced her by sending her Joan Baez's *Diamonds and Rust,* and then she invited him to her house, where they lay in front of her fireplace and listened to that album over and over.

That means, Delores, that every time they wanted to listen to the record again, one of them had to get up off the floor and walk over to the record player and pick up the needle—or flip the record and *then* pick up the needle—and place it ever so gently onto the spinning LP.

It's old-school birth control? Oh, Delores, you should tweet that. Not now, for heaven's sake!

If we were at Jane's, she'd put Delores's iPhone in her blender. It's the horror reader in her. Jane loves to provoke a blood-curdling scream.

Book Club rotates apartments and house rules apply. So, that means no cell phones at Jane's and no gum chewing here. There's no red wine at Bethany's. At Marjorie's, don't pretend to hunt for an extra box of Cheese Nips so you can search out her jars. The ladies on the red sofa make you take off your shoes. The ladies on the gray sofa make you keep your shoes on. Delores lives with me, so it's in her best interest that you do what I say.

Honestly, for Delores to remain a member of Book Club, dear, it's imperative that you become a member.

And you want to stay in Book Club, don't you, Delores?

Yes, Delores knows: as long as you take care of Book Club, Book Club takes care of you.

When Delores found herself in a transitional period, like the one you're in now, dear, she was eighteen, orphaned and penniless because her dead mother hadn't worked for a generous company like Talbots. So, I took her in. And because Delores's mother was a member of Book Club, Book Club sent Delores to Smith. We visit Jane at Mount Sinai when she has her strokes. We set Bethany up on blind dates. We ignore Marjorie's hormonal mood swings. The ladies on the red sofa babysit for Aretha. As a matter of fact, so do the ladies on the gray sofa because Aretha can't find paid professionals willing to cope with all of her kids.

Aretha's the glassy-eyed woman scooping Bethany's store-bought potato salad into her hand. She came to Book Club through Marjorie, who makes her sales targets every quarter because Aretha—to escape her kids—spends an inordinate amount of time shopping at Talbots.

Aretha's fertility specialist hit it out of the park. Twins: two sets, two years apart.

Aretha's fertility specialist also happens to be her husband. He's got the highest insemination success rate in the country, but Marjorie won't go near him. Neither will the ladies on the red sofa. The ladies on the gray sofa will resort to using him only if their acupuncture and herbal immersion tanks fail. At the hospital, Bethany says Aretha's husband's nickname is Dr. Uh-Oh. He'll get you pregnant, but far too often messes up the details.

For example: Aretha's ten-year-olds have her blue eyes and their father's curly hair, but one is a screamer and the other has to wear a football helmet 24/7 because in order to communicate he has to shake his head like a bottle of Snapple. If you look directly at either one of them, they'll charge you like lions on the Serengeti. If you look directly at Aretha's eight-year-olds, they too will take it as an act of aggression, but plot your come-uppance for when you least expect it. Once, they slipped crushed Ritalin into my Pinot. They're lurkers. Always mushrooming up amid living room furniture like clammy ottomans. At Aretha's, Book Club resembles a bunch of actresses playing blind, affixing our lines of sight on distant spots and groping for crudité. But it's so hard not to look at her eight-year-olds, because Dr. Uh-Oh's slapdash juggling of vials made them unmistakably Hispanic.

As a courtesy, Bethany diagnosed Aretha's eight-year-olds as borderline psychotic. Jane calls them "a handful."

Two handfuls? Oh Aretha, how you manage to keep your sense of humor I do not know!

Oh, yes I do, dear. Dr. Uh-Oh keeps Aretha highly medicated. You know the saying: happy wife, happy life? Dr. Uh-Oh's mantra is: you asked for it, muddle through. Like the majority of his patients, Aretha gave birth in her forties. She defied God's will, she shouldn't complain.

Aretha likes Book Club to read Southern Gothics because in them children like hers fall easily by the wayside. In Southern Gothics, there is no difference between a slow reader and a serial killer. There are no spectrums, learning or otherwise. If a boy "ain't right," he's institutionalized. Or some sense is slapped into him. Or he's confined to a room or a shed or a silo. Or he's allowed to wander down to the swamp to poke a gator with a stick. In Southern Gothics, disease weeds out the weak. One bout of dysentery, and it's poo-poo to you!

You must try one of my bacon-wrapped water chestnuts, dear.

Delores, bring us the platter of bacon-wrapped water chestnuts, please and thank you!

Dip it in the spicy sauce, dear. The secret ingredient is mayonnaise.

In addition to being an amazing cook, I read everything. And I have the time to do so because I don't have children. I'm fortunate enough to have found a husband who agrees with me that not having children means that the two of us can have nothing but fun. And, to me, fun is Book Club.

Honestly, there is nothing I will not do to be the very best hostess.

If you agree to join Book Club, Jane will let you live in one of her empty rooms, perhaps the one next to the terrarium, and she will pay off every cent of your debt. Under Bethany's watchful eye, Dr. Uh-Oh will perform your first insemination, for which Jane will pay you handsomely. And I mean, George Clooney handsomely.

You'll surrogate Marjorie's baby first because she's suffered the most losses. Then Bethany's, because by that point she'll be ready to embrace the fact that having it all can be just a couple of things and one of those things doesn't have to be birthed the old-fashioned way. The ladies on the red sofa will draw straws to decide who uses you next. The ladies on the gray sofa will play rock-paper-scissors. And then—only if you are physically able, my dear—Aretha would appreciate a do-over.

I will be in charge of blackmailing her husband.

Oh, don't look so surprised, dear. Win, lose, or jars, we'll never reject you like that ex-husband of yours.

Delores knows this from firsthand experience. Her

mother swore Delores was as fertile as a Duggar, so we took her into our fold with great expectations, but we all know how that turned out. A twisted uterus can't catch.

You, dear, I have a feeling, will be better than gift bags.

So what do you say? I have an extra Talbots bunny brooch that would love to curl up on your shoulder. I've got my laminating machine and hole-punch ready to tassel your bookmark. Have you thought of a Book Club name? Do try and stay away from mine, Mary Beth. Don't pick Mary Alice or Elizabeth. May I make a suggestion?

With that crooked smile, you look like a Hadley.

THE FITTER

The Fitter is mine. Myrtle Babcock can get her flabby pancake tits out of his face. He's sizing her up in her ill-fitting turtleneck that's off-white and thin because it's been through the wash too many times. Her "nude" athletic bra shows through like she's smuggling ferrets. Here's what, sister: every woman needs underwire, and when you stuff two pounds of downed rounds into A-cups, beige ain't invisible.

The Fitter doesn't touch her. He shakes his head no when she offers to lift her top.

I say, "This ain't Mardi Gras, Myrtle."

The Fitter waves his hand for me to be quiet. He leans forward in his recliner.

My husband, the Fitter, looks like every other middle-aged man in this small Georgia town. Somehow skinny and fat. Always in khakis with a nice enough smile. He talks like everybody else. He says, "Yes, ma'am" and "No, sir." He mows his own lawn. He passes the collection plate at church. If you saw him at the gas station, you wouldn't do more than say hello. But you'd be missing out. The Fitter is a wonder.

Like some men are born with an ear for music or a brain for math, the Fitter was born with an appraiser's eye. Before he could crawl, he knew that square pegs belonged in square holes. In preschool, he packed his backpack so that it sat like a nut in a shell inside his cubby. A Little Leaguer, he worked his catcher's mitt so that the ball stuck every time that he caught it. His mother had him stuff all her deviled eggs.

When the Fitter turned twelve, his father let him in on the family secret: his grandfather was a fitter; his great-grandfather was a fitter. The Fitter's own father had bowed out of the business because he blushed like a fire hydrant. That and he would have taken over the family trade in the 1970s when bras were historically at their least popular. The Fitter's father drove him to Atlanta and walked him through Macy's bra department. The Fitter was shorter than the racks. Padding grazed his cheeks and salesladies raised their eyebrows, but he never turned red. He listened to his father talk about bras like they were nests in the woods. Every nest fits a couple. All couples are to be respected and admired from afar. No two pairs are exactly the same.

A female security guard was called to escort the Fitter and his father out of the bra department, and on their way out, the Fitter plucked a Playtex 18 Hour Original from a rack and offered it to her. They were still kicked out of Macy's, but the guard later tried on the bra. Salesladies peered over the dressing room door, clutched the measuring tapes that draped their necks like ropes of pearls, and marveled. In the course of two minutes the woman had transformed from Lurch Addams to Jane Russell.

Word spread. An urban legend was born. There's this kid who's part good old boy, part miracle worker. When the Fitter turned eighteen, he opened his doors for business. Cars backed up the highway like there was a new mall.

The Fitter is what you call pilgrimage-worthy. He sees you, he sells to you, and you leave with your breasts and your spirits soaring higher than kites. A good bra is fine, but a great bra is life changing. It gives you the confidence of a homecoming queen. It's a tiara for your ta-tas. Rich women from big cities—as big as New York City—gather up their book clubs and fly Delta to Atlanta and charter limos to drive them down Highway 85 to a lake road to our porch. Myrtle is a local, on the saggy side of forty, and I know what it's taken for her to finally knock on our door.

Myrtle arches her back, offering her sad state of affairs like a teller offers bags of cash in a bank heist.

The Fitter waves his hand.

I say, "That means back up, Myrtle. Stand like you normally stand." I think: Like you've been waiting in line for an hour at the 7-Eleven and now the Slurpee machine's broke.

The Fitter says, "34C."

Myrtle says, "No!"

"Yes," says the Fitter.

To me he says, "Pull her three styles: a full-coverage, a plunging neckline, and a balcony. None beige. Get her the Gilligan's Island special: the hardworking girl next door, Marie Jo, and her fancy friend, Chantelle. Pull her the one that means 'royal subjects' in Norwegian—the pink one with the tulips on the straps. Show this nice lady that there's life after Maidenform."

Myrtle squeals and claps her hands. Her breasts flap like empty pantyhose legs. She follows me down the hall of our house to the dressing room, our master bath.

Before I shut the door on her, I say, "Don't get any funny ideas."

She says, "What on earth are you implying?"

I say, "That right there: those airs. It has all been

done, Myrtle. Love notes in the medicine cabinet, panties under his brown towel. Just last week, those women from down at the YWCA showed up in their two-pieces and ran through our sprinklers. But he married me and he married me a long time ago. As long as I draw breath, nobody—including you—is getting the Fitter."

Myrtle huffs and plops down on the toilet.

I leave her and go to our bedroom walk-in closet.

It is a forest of bras. The Fitter orders them from London. He orders them from France. He orders them from anywhere you might see someone's underpants. All those mini-hangers you see in department stores? The Fitter had pencil-wide closet rods custom-built for them. There are fifteen rows running floor to ceiling, covering three walls. Rods for the most gargantuan of what can only be referred to as *brassieres* run across the ceiling. The cups are as menacing as cauldrons of boiling oil.

I squat to comb the rack of C cups at my knees.

My equilibrium is shot because of what those women from down at the hospital have been putting me through, but I catch my balance and surf the carpet. I'm a good employee. I'm the only employee and I want to keep it that way. So I'll pull Myrtle the best, what the Fitter has asked me to pull: specifically the pink princess bra with tulips that costs $125. But that will be the cheapest by far.

Marie Jo and Chantelle run from $88 up and I'll choose the *up*. I'll make Myrtle pay for her flirting with her entire Kroger's two-week paycheck. I come out with three bras totaling $443.

The Fitter sits on the edge of our bed.

Myrtle is hanging her head and shoulders out from behind the bathroom door, telling him how much she likes the kimono she's wearing. The kimono is a genuine kimono ordered all the way from Japan. The Fitter has six. All silk. All colors you don't see anywhere in these parts. The Fitter likes his customers to have a taste of the exotic. His theory is: if a woman is treated well, she'll spend money like she's treated that well all the time. The kimono Myrtle is wearing is covered in cranes and hibiscus. It's the same one I wore when the Fitter's first wife fitted me.

Myrtle is braless. I had no idea her breasts could descend any farther with her bra off, but by God, they most certainly can. Her nipples peek out from behind the door like eavesdroppers.

The Fitter waves his hand.

I say, "Myrtle, in with you. He's ready. Let's go."

Myrtle shuffles backward into the bathroom.

Her turtleneck is slung across my vanity table. My guess is that she's tucked the bra she came in with into her purse. I imagine a loose Lifesaver adhering to the nylon. Women never think to hang their things on the fancy peg where they took the kimono. I shut the door in disgust and hang the bras on the towel rack. Myrtle tolerates my curtness because she's heard tell of what will happen now that we're alone.

From the bedroom, the Fitter says, "Start with the basic."

I take the full-coverage off the hanger and unhook the triple clips. The bra is black with a baby blue satin ribbon between the cups. I hold the straps with my hands in the ten-and-two position.

Myrtle drops the kimono to land in a puddle at her bare feet. There is no reason she should have taken off her jeans, socks, and shoes. It's a fitting, not a pelvic exam. When I pick up the kimono, I see she's painted her toes. Had them painted, more likely. No one can do a French pedicure right on her own feet. A French pedicure is an investment. A French pedicure is what some women get to go on their honeymoons. When the Fitter and I went on our honeymoon, I had my toenails painted red. Red is what good wives wear. French pedicures make your toes look like fingers. You look grabby. French pedicures are for man thieves.

I say, "Who did your toes, Myrtle? That maroon-headed know-it-all down at the blow-out shop you call a mother?"

Myrtle says, "Barbara sends her love."

"Barbara doesn't know me."

Barbara is the manicurist where I get my wig fixed. I've had to wear that wig for a good part of a year now, and I've learned that if I don't get it washed and styled once a week, the top of my head looks like something has crawled up on it, had a seizure, and died. No matter what time I make an appointment, from opening to close, Barbara is ever present at her nail station, gossiping at a volume loud enough to carry over three hair dryers while she dunks hands of all ages into paraffin wax. When my wig comes off, Barbara and her customers practice the Southern Lady art of staring without overtly staring. But I can feel their eyes like hot-from-the-dryer fabric softener sheets stuck to my clothes. They each cling to the hope that one of them will take my place.

Because the Fitter is richer than any man they've ever met. And he's humbler. He has one truck, one fishing boat, and one house. And he's devoted. He has one shop and one wife. Barbara and her customers want the regular beauty parlor appointments that being that wife afford me. Except Barbara wants this for her daughter.

Now that she's sent Myrtle here, I must look worse than I think.

I don't like Barbara. And I don't like her daughter

because I don't trust any woman who calls her mother by her first name.

Myrtle says, "Don't leave me hanging."

I can't help myself: I say, "Good one."

I present the bra like a straitjacket, and Myrtle slips her arms through the straps.

And then my hands are on her breasts. That's just the way it is. I don't think about whom I'm handling, I just handle her. I scoop. I pour. I pack. I hook. I adjust straps. Not too tight, but tight enough to leave a mark. I'm fast. I get Myrtle locked and loaded before she can blink.

The Fitter says, "Well?"

Myrtle looks in the full-length mirror on the back of the bathroom door. She pivots. She gapes. Her breasts sit above her rib cage.

"Oh, thank you!" she cries to him. "Thank you, thank you!"

The Fitter says, "Hop."

Myrtle looks to me and I nod. I hate it when they hop. When they hop, every woman is a sixteen-year-old girl. Myrtle hops and for the first time in a long, long time her breasts don't *boing* like Slinkies.

"Oh!" she cries.

The Fitter says, "See there."

"Oh, I do! Thank you! I do I do I do!"

Myrtle will not shut up about what the Fitter has done

for her because women love men who excel at their craft. More so, they love men who are faithful. And what's more faithful than a married fitter who doesn't touch, much less *look* at another woman's breasts?

The Fitter is quiet. He lets Myrtle's gratitude warm our once hothouse of a home. Without me hawking over him, I know he lets himself smile. He knows Myrtle is so in awe of her transformation that she'll reach for her reflection in the mirror on her side of the door. If she's crazy bold, she'll reach for the knob. There is a chance I won't stop her.

But, I do.

I whisper, "Careful, Myrtle. The Fitter don't cheat."

He didn't call *me* until his first wife, his high school girlfriend, ran away with the falsies distributor. Since then he won't stock falsies. Won't even look at one: cotton/polyester blend or bags of saline. He swears he loves me the way I am now after my surgery, but I ache for what I had. Why his first wife couldn't have fallen in love with the nipple tape guy is beyond me.

The Fitter calls, "Next."

I choose the balcony bra. It's lavender-and-gold stretch lace with aerodynamic support. It's meant to hike your breasts up like corsets used to do. You get all of the *oomph* with none of the *ouch*. We in the business call it the Cleavage Maker.

I bend Myrtle over at the waist and drop her breasts into the demi cups like muffin batter. When she rises, those muffins are baked. Myrtle marvels and pats the tops.

The Fitter says, "I don't hear anything."

Myrtle opens her mouth, but catches sight of my face.

I know my color's gone. The side effects from my "aggressive" treatment grab me out of nowhere and make me want to barf.

I reach out for the toilet, but it's Myrtle's arm I catch on the way to the floor.

Myrtle rests my back against the bathtub. She calls out, "The bra's fine."

"Fine?" says the Fitter. "I've never heard just fine."

"It's beautiful," calls Myrtle. She runs cold faucet water over a washcloth. "Magic." She tips my head between my knees and lays the cool cloth on the back of my neck. She calls, "I've never felt more like a woman."

She winces at her faux pas. She looks at me like, *Oops. My bad.*

I wave one of the Fitter's waves. This one means, *Forget it.*

The Fitter is a man of few words, but the ones he speaks outside of day-to-day dealings are all compliments. When I came for my first fitting, he had his first wife pull a 36DD with modesty padding because he said

I had a body meant for tight sweaters. When we married, he filled my dresser with cashmere crewnecks because he said I deserved to wear nice things. In bed, he's said it's my giggling that drives him wild. At work, he's said I'm tireless, a model, and great with customers.

But none of this is true anymore.

Sweaters swallow me. Insomnia drives me to spend nights on the couch. I won't deserve Employee of the Year this year—Myrtle can attest to that.

I say to her, "I wasn't always this jealous."

She says, "You're right to be jealous."

"Goddammit." I pull off the washcloth. I wring it like I've wanted to wring so many customers' necks. I throw the washcloth into a corner.

Myrtle fishes an open Lifesaver roll from her purse. She frowns as she pulls it out because the green one is— as I predicted—stuck to her Old Yeller of a bra. She offers me the orange at the top of the roll.

I refuse.

She says, "One of us is going to get him. You might as well let me be nice to you." She unwinds the foil string, pops the orange in her mouth, and offers me the cherry.

I take it. And of course it tastes good. Red is always the best flavor. It takes the bitterness out of my mouth.

The Fitter calls, "What's the holdup?"

When we don't answer, I hear the bedsprings squeak. The Fitter walks toward the bathroom door. He knocks. He's never knocked.

He asks, "Is everything okay in there?"

And then to Myrtle: "Is she okay?"

"I'm fine," I answer.

But I know I'm not fine. The sicker I get, the more business booms.

I reach out and let Myrtle help me to my feet. I take the last bra—the pink princess bra—from the towel rack. Myrtle takes off the balcony. Her breasts droop. They look sad. The pink princess bra is happy. I hold it out for her to slip her arms through, but Myrtle doesn't budge. She stares at the appliqué tulips on the straps.

She admits, "I can't afford it."

"You could charge it."

"Barbara won't let me have any debt."

Myrtle pulls her not-so-sporty sports bra over her head. She gathers herself. Her tamped-down nipples look like googly eyes.

I say, "You'll keep your mom from gossiping? You'll keep the other women in line?"

Myrtle nods.

"You'll be nice?"

She picks up my washcloth. She folds it and places it on the edge of the sink. She puts the balcony and the basic back on their hangers. She spreads the kimono so that its cranes look like they will fly off the peg.

None of this is done as I would do it, but I wave my hand: *Good enough.*

I slip the pink bra into her purse.

HOW TO BE A

GROWN-ASS LADY

Compliment everyone. Take a compliment. Wear sunscreen on your face and hands even when it's cloudy. Dye your gray hair black, brown, or blond. Run the dishwasher half full. Have company over and serve what you want to eat. When a guest says your meat loaf looks like a football, don't tell the woman that her husband is obviously gay.

Don't bite your cuticles. Get rid of a wart before there's a cluster. Don't sit on a toilet in front of anyone, ever. If your husband wants a bigger TV, for heaven's sake let him have it.

Go to the mall for your Clinique bonus gift. Buy three pieces of clothing twice a year at full price. Get refitted for bras on your birthday. Replace your tights every winter. Forget thongs. If your white shirt has sweat stains, throw it away. Tip 20 percent on the whole bill including alcohol and tax. When St. Jude's mails you personalized address labels and asks for a forty-five-dollar donation, write them a check.

Get your Pap smears and mammograms. Get your teeth cleaned. Join a book club. Join two. Never put your phone on a restaurant table. Don't tell your friends with kids that if they die, you'll take care of their kids.

If you don't like something someone says, say: "That's interesting."

If you like something someone says, say: "That's interesting!"

Don't brag about not going to church. Don't complain about your interior designer. Give flight attendants your full attention during their in-case-of-emergency take-off routines. Talk to cabdrivers. Engage strangers while waiting in line.

Don't reprimand people who call you sweetheart.

Don't reprimand people who call you ma'am.

Accept it: you're too old to drink more than one drink and sleep through the night. Face it: you're never going to get carded again, so quit asking bouncers if they want to see your ID. Quit going places where they have bouncers.

Call friends you haven't spoken to since high school and tell them about your weird dream that they were in. Don't chastise your husband because he dream-cheated on you. When your husband is in the bathroom, don't knock on or talk to him through the closed bathroom door. When a young person doesn't get your reference, don't repeat, "Kiss my grits!" with the hope that they will.

Call people under thirty kids.

Call people over sixty young.

Listen to gangsta rap in the privacy of your own headphones. Listen to erotic audiobooks when you scrub the bathroom floor. Worry about cancer. Google menopause. Challenge insurance claims. Ask your friend who's a shrink if you should see a shrink. Don't look at your profile because it's not the mirror or the lighting or the time of day, it's you.

HOW TO BE A PATRON

OF THE ARTS

Step 1: Take your husband's money.

He will offer it to you six years after your first novel is published. You refused to marry him until that first novel sold. Then you spent those six years writing a second novel while you held on to your secretarial job so you wouldn't get a big head about your literary success or lose yourself in marriage. Your literary success was three reprints and a spot in *Vogue*'s "What People Are Talking About." Marriage is a soft place full of three-thousand-dollar couches and twenty-eight-dollar bottles of wine.

You write on weekends because you work in an office fifty hours a week because you need something to fall back on and you don't want to fall back on your husband. So you take dictation, make appointments; you juggle phone lines, you open mail. You point to signature lines while your book advance dwindles. If you don't finish your word-count quota, you don't go out with friends. And you never go on vacation, and you haven't had kids. You'll do all that once your second novel is published. But it hasn't been published because you haven't gotten it right.

"Writing is rewriting," you tell your husband.

He says, "I can't stand to see you like this."

You are hunched over your desk and wearing your pajamas. The cats bat at your drawstrings. You sneeze and powdered sugar from a doughnut comes out your nose. You haven't had sex since forever because your failings are armor. Cross your legs and you clink.

Your husband says, "Let me support you and you can just write."

When he opens the blinds to let in the afternoon light, cover your face and nod. Cry because it hurts.

Step 2: Lose yourself in marriage.

Quit your secretarial job and realize how much easier it is to take care of only one man, especially when that one man, your husband, has a secretary of his own. Be grateful for this gift of uninterrupted writing time and show your husband how grateful you are.

Clean the apartment like you've never cleaned an apartment. Buy a bristled wand that gets the dust out of the radiator. Buy a fuzzy claw on a stick to get at the molding. Buy a toothbrush that's not a toothbrush that gets grime out from around the oven dials. Repaint the place. Bright colors—Hanna-Barbera Yellow! Breakfast at Tiffany's Blue! Not Your Grandmother's Coral!—so that your apartment looks like a slice of Key West on the Upper East Side. Buy a new three-thousand-dollar couch because the cats turned the old one into a scratching post. Have people over. For dinner. For Oscar night. For board games. To play poker. Entertain. Cater everything all by yourself.

Say thank you when friends say, "You should be a party planner!"

Make love to your husband when he says, "Wasn't tonight fun?"

Make love to your husband sometimes two times a week. Remember what a good kisser he is. Touch places and perform acts that he wouldn't want you to write that you touched and performed. Enjoy the embarrassment. Learn that life's more fun when you're loose.

Step 3: Make your own mantra.

Take Pilates. Take hot yoga. Take restorative yoga where you wrap your arms and legs around a bolster like a treed koala bear for forty minutes. Walk around the Reservoir. Walk past crusties and chuggers and upskirters and stale MILFs. Plow through herds of private-school track team girls like a chafe-resistant crop-panted Lululemon-wearing Moses.

For as long as you can remember, writing has been your religion. So, play God. Think up a new and improved list of writing commandments:

Thou shalt not put your writing before your health.
Thou shalt not compare your writing schedule to
    Stephen King's.
Thou shalt not curse those published in *Tin House*.
Thou shalt remember that you published one novel
    and that is more than most people do.
Thou shalt write a monthly check to Sallie Mae to
    pay off your student loan and not make a fuss
    about it.
Thou shalt kill your darlings.
Thou shalt not beat yourself up for not writing any
    darlings.
Thou shalt not plagiarize just to get the ball rolling.
Thou shalt not lie that you are "working on some-
    thing."
Thou shalt not envy those who really are.

Step 4: Support the literary community.

When you come upon the independent bookstore, stand back and marvel. Touch a lamppost to steady your balance. It's like you've found a unicorn grazing next to the dry cleaner that a friend told you could get cat barf out of cashmere. Inside, the woman behind the counter wears glasses, two pairs at once. She's a regular six-eyes. She's in a caftan. Or is that a muumuu? Whichever, the bell sleeves could ring in the New Year.

"Can I help you?" she asks.

"Just looking," you say.

Half a dozen stuffed ravens circle you from the tops of bookshelves. Their marble eyeballs are cloudy. You reach into your purse and finger your Wet Wipes. A clock strikes noon and an automated voice squawks, "The butler did it! The butler did it!"

You ask, "What does the clock say at one?"

She says, "It's always the butler. You're in a mystery bookstore. The joke never gets old."

You don't read mysteries, but this lady and her talking clock and her dead birds make you want to give it a whirl. You ask, "What would you suggest?"

She asks, "Do you have any hobbies?"

You don't want to say writing, so you say, "Poker."

She says, "Try the Short Stacked series." She motions

to a display table piled with mass-market paperbacks. She says, "It's about a woman poker player who's four foot nine, flat-chested, and broke. She travels the tournament circuit and has all kinds of weird poker player friends. The first one takes place at the Aviation Club in Paris. A dealer goes missing, so it's called *Button, Button, Who's Got the Button?*"

Buy the book at full price so the writer gets her full royalty of fifty-nine cents and the independent bookstore gets a cut that will help it stay afloat in a choppy sea of pirated e-books. Carry your paperback proudly like a public radio tote bag. Show it off on the subway and in line for bank tellers. Read the mystery book. Guess who did it and be delighted when you're wrong. Go back to the store and buy the next one in the series. Read and repeat until you've read all ten Short Stacked books, ending with *Dead Donkeys Don't Rabbit Hunt.* Rejoice in this new world outside the masterpiece opus that you've been struggling to write.

Attend Malice Domestic, a conference for mysteries in which mostly female protagonists have pet cats that never die and an eye for clues that police don't pick up on. Share a hotel room with your new friend, the independent bookstore lady, whose name is Joyce. Meet writers and readers who, just like Joyce, have draped their postmenopausal torsos with colorful sheaths and heaped chunky necklaces up their throats like Fisher-Price ring tosses. Share online clothes catalog links. Share pictures of your cats. This one looks like they're reading the newspaper. Meet the Short Stacked novelist, who dresses her twenty-pound calico like different literary detectives and photographs him for her annual fan calendar. For 2016, with the help of a granny wig and a disbelieving glower, Miss Marple is July.

Volunteer to host a fund-raiser to save Joyce's struggling independent bookstore. Ask mystery writers you met at Malice Domestic to donate works of art to be sold. The Short Stacked author donates a calico portrait of Jack Reacher sitting in a bathroom sink. Joyce parts with one of her ravens, which it turns out she had stuffed by her former attorney-turned-taxidermist, who runs her business out of a Classic Six on Fifth and Sixty-Third.

Amass fifty pieces. Hang them on your apartment walls. Place the raven on your writing desk that you'll use for writing once this fund-raiser is over. Make a price sheet and overcharge. Invite poker players from your weekly game. Invite alumni from your graduate creative writing program who now have kids, teaching gigs, two novels published, or all of the above. Invite Joyce to invite her best customers. Invite author art donors to invite a plus one. Serve Poirot Punch—a mixture of strawberry Kool-Aid and Prosecco—to get everyone drunk. Serve pigs-in-blankets you've crafted to look like severed fingers to make everyone thirsty so that they drink more. When somebody buys something, mark the wall beside it with a red sticker dot. Red sticker dots make people crazy. They're contagious and everybody wants one and wants one right now.

"It's bedlam!" cries a gentleman in orange corduroys.

There is a buying frenzy and your walls get the measles.

Say thank you when friends say, "You should open an art gallery!"

Make love to your husband after he buys the one piece that wasn't bought, Joyce's raven.

Step 5: Become a gay man's arm candy.

When Clive Lee phones to ask you to lunch, say yes. Clive Lee is the gentleman who wore the orange cords and bought the cat in the sink picture for two thousand dollars. He is also an editor at Berkley Prime Crime.

Meet him at Michael's, a warhorse of literary lunch spots where your Scribner editor met you six years ago to celebrate, but never took you again because you never came through with book number two. Cradle a dirty vodka martini and pick at a Cobb salad and gobble up

Clive Lee's gossip about every publishing hotshot and MacArthur genius that walks through the door.

Wish you were a MacArthur genius.

Clive Lee asks, "Why, so you can spend the rest of your miserable born days trying to live up to your potential?"

Shrug. Mash an avocado cube with your fork.

Clive Lee says, "Madam, you are a lady of the house. You are a woman of leisure. That is all anyone in their right mind wants to be."

Go to lunch with Clive Lee once a week. Go to book parties with him. Go to book award banquets with him. Go to the opera and Encores! and Carnegie Hall. Attend Broadway and Off-Broadway and black box performances with foldout chairs in the depths of downtown. Start applause. Rattle your jewelry. Rejoice in your discovery that gay men love middle-aged women with no kids, cash, and time on their hands. Every time you sit down to write, accept an invitation for something more fabulous to do.

Teach eight of Clive Lee's friends to play poker on Sunday nights in the orchestra pit of *The Book of Mormon*. Bank $3K monthly off a violinist who, despite your teachings, always pushes all-in with the second-best hand.

Say thank you when Clive Lee says, "You should be a professional poker player!"

Make love to your husband when he says, "It's your money. Do whatever you want with it."

Step 6: Buy art.

Go to the Affordable Art Fair, Scope, Red Dot, Volta, and Pulse, where artists are "emerging." "Emerging" in Manhattan means less than ten grand. Buy a Doe. Buy a Ball. Buy Emilie Clark and Frohawk Two Feathers. Buy an ape head made of tinfoil. Buy a slide projector that projects the word "SUCKAH" on your bedroom wall. Think better of this placement and move the projector to your kitchen. Link your arm with Joyce's and visit School of Visual Arts students' work spaces in abandoned can factories and naval yards located twelve blocks from any subway stop in Brooklyn. Get to know Dumbo. Brave Bushwick. Buy a photo of a Cracker Barrel robber with a pantie on his head. Commission a photo of your medicine cabinet that Clive Lee tells you is the Warhol screen print of today. Trust your own taste and commission the tinfoil artist to craft sculptures of your cats.

Place the tinfoil cats next to Joyce's raven on your writing desk. Remove your laptop because it interrupts the visual flow. Plug it in on the kitchen counter and use it to Pinterest recipes for a dinner party in the tinfoil artist's honor. Beam with pride when Clive Lee and three other guests ask for seconds and buy tinfoil ape heads for their art collections.

Accept the tinfoil artist's extra-long handsy hug.

Say thank you when the tinfoil artist says, "You should be a nude model!"

Make love to your husband when he says, "Over my dead body."

Step 7: Become a muse.

Let the tinfoil artist sculpt your head and chest from the cleavage up. This is his first foray into the human form and it earns him an exhibition at Morgan Lehman Gallery, and nine versions of your tinfoil self sell out in twenty minutes. His art student friends get the shakes from the red sticker dots. They're all starving and look even hungrier in their hand-painted high-tops. They are sprite-like and travel in a clump. They come at you like your cats do when you unwrap deli meat. Their energy is frenetic. Bend down and say hello.

When asked what you do, say, "I'm just a fan."

When pressed, try: "I'm a housewife."

When pressed further (as in: yes, but what did you do *before* you got married?), admit that you published one book. "It was a novel." Talk about it in the past tense as if it's a dead child. Don't lie. Obey your commandments. Say, "I'm not working on anything now." Don't lie. Say, "I'm into helping young artists."

A videographer asks, "Would you help me?"

"And me?" asks a young lady whose handmade hat looks like an anatomically correct heart.

Say, "Sure."

Wear the heart girl's kidney fascinator to the Met Costume Ball. When asked, give the hat and the girl's information to Anna Wintour. Be okay with the fact that now *Vogue* is talking about the organ hat artist. Show how okay you are by placing her issue on the top of your coffee table's fanned array of magazines.

Take an Ambien and let the videographer record you sleeping in pearls and an apron in front of your cats on your kitchen floor. The Ambien gives you night terrors and makes the cats jump. Over the course of the fast-forwarded video that wins him a spot in the Whitney Biennial, watch yourself scream and kick your legs in a cloud of shed fur.

Say thank you when a Whitney curator says, "You should be on our board!"

Make love to your husband when he says, "Madam Chairman might beat out my fantasy of acid-wash jeans rocker chick."

Step 8: Develop a signature look.

Grow your hair shoulder length and clip it at the base of your neck with a barrette. Clive Lee says this is seventies chic.

He says, "It's so simple. So Jackie O."

Buy a pair of green-rimmed sunglasses that when you're indoors always perch on your head. Wear only sheath dresses. Never wear a cardigan no matter how cold it is. Never wear pantyhose. Leave your jewelry at home. Short red nails are your best accessories. Stilettos are for women with nowhere to go.

Your signature look says: I have good taste. I am confident. You can trust me. Let me help.

People know you when they see you. Lit mag and museum interns copy your style. Gallery owners push through crowds to air kiss your cheeks. They remember you drink dirty martinis and offer to have their girl (who is doing her darnedest to look forty and fabulous) fetch you one with extra olives. Everyone asks you what to see, when to go, how to get tickets, who you're reading, and where to shop. They want to look like and live like and be just like you.

You don't blame them.

Ask your husband, "Will you still love me if I quit writing for good?"

Make love to him, no matter what he says.

DEAD DOORMEN

B eing a wife is a commitment.

I get up before my husband. I pour coffee from the coffeemaker and pull sliced melon from the fridge. I place the melon on family china. I place the plate on an antique tray. I serve my husband breakfast in bed. Well, maybe *serve* isn't the word I'm supposed to use in this day and age, but I don't know what else I would call it. Bring? I bring my husband coffee, melon, and toast.

When the tray touches his lap, my husband winds my bathrobe tie around his hand and kisses me for as long as he likes. My husband is groggy and grateful. It is my only kiss of the day.

When my husband's at work, I don't get lonely. I have plenty to do. There's the dusting. And in the city, the dust never stops. To mop, polish, or disinfect, the dust has to go first. To have anyone into this apartment, the apartment has to be clean.

John, the Irish doorman, says, "It's amazing you're able to keep this place up by yourself. Your husband's mother had staff—a laundress and a cook—although she never could keep a maid. All the girls quit because they were expected to keep this place like a museum."

I say, "There's nothing wrong with having nice things."

When I met my husband's mother, she spilled red wine on her cream-colored rug. Before she rang a service bell, I was on my knees with a bottle of cleanser I kept in my purse. My husband protested. Staff hurried in at the sound of his voice, but my husband's mother waved them off. She bent forward, clutched her two-toned cardigan, and marveled at how the stain dabbed up on my napkin.

She said to my husband, "This one's quick. Prepared. Appreciative. Thorough. She'll get rid of a mess before you can make it."

She asked me: "How old are you? Are your parents still with you? Are you good in the kitchen? Do you have a career?"

I answered.

She nodded.

He nodded.

I did, too.

The next day, her five-carat engagement ring appeared on my finger.

A year later, she was dead, her domestics fired, and I was the lady of my husband's mother's prewar penthouse.

I can clean, but I can't fix things. That's the beauty of a co-op. We have eighteen doormen, a handyman, and a super. I don't like to bother the handyman for small jobs, so when something like my radio goes on the fritz, John the doorman appears.

John's been with the building since my husband was a boy. He's a permanent fixture, like the gargoyle that juts out under our living room window. The thing's cement head is as cool as John's temperament. The man never gets rattled. He never ages. My husband has a black-and-white photo of John teaching him to ride a bike under our awning's TAXI light. John looks sixty in that photo and he looks sixty today.

The broken radio is in my kitchen, which is the only room in this four-bedroom apartment that for now I call my own. It's been modernized because appliances die and must be replaced. I replace them—the blender, the mixer—with what I can afford off the Internet with my debit card allowance.

I saved eight years for a commercial chest freezer.

I have an unpainted wooden stool that John gave me after I moved in because he knew that, like my husband's mother's cook, I'd have no place to sit. The kitchen stool is plain compared to every other Victorian piece of furniture that resides in our house, but I like it because John gave it to me and it keeps my weight off my feet.

My husband's mother didn't like anyone in her home getting too comfortable. Well, maybe "comfortable" isn't the word I should use to reveal her true nature. She meant lazy.

She told me, "Lazy people cut corners. They slack. They infringe."

When her six-year-old son, my husband, ate cookies in bed, she shipped him off to boarding school. He spent summers at sleepaway camp. He went to college and wasn't allowed to move back into this apartment until he got engaged. I don't think either one of them thought it would take as long as it did to find me: a wife who could and *would* take care of her things.

My husband's a slob.

Every morning he ignores the saucer on his breakfast tray and places his coffee cup on the oak bedside table. He wipes his jelly knife on the edge of the tray. He shakes his napkin over the sheets. He's wiped his mouth on the coverlet monogram.

And so, after he goes to work, the tray and the sheets go to soak in the side-by-side kitchen sinks.

The kitchen is my office, like my husband's midtown floor of suites is his. In all these years of marriage, I have never laid eyes on one of his secretaries. He's never poured himself a glass of milk. I couldn't tell you the color of his desk blotter. He doesn't know that I have a stool or a radio or that I have John.

The radio in John's hands blares Hot 97 FM and I jump.

John smiles as if he meant to goose me. He says, "Your problem is your thingamajig. Your thingamajig's loose and needs to be tighter in your whatchamacallit."

I offer John my wooden stool.

He doesn't take it. He'd never sit while on the clock.

He holds my radio to his ear and twists the dial. Static hums like the party an apartment like this expects.

We only host co-op board meetings. Hosting anything bigger would be too much of a mess.

My husband is the co-op board president like my husband's mother was the co-op board president before him. Every three months, members gather around our cocktail table and whisper as if the wall sconces are bugged. A co-op is managed by money, but more so by gossip. Divorce, senility, bed bugs, leaks. The board knows all. And its president must decide what to do and then do it.

My husband's mother took every step to ensure that her rule would continue. She made her son, my husband, balance the building's books. She made him fire the building's most beloved and senior employee. She made me aware of what part I should play.

She told me, "The board trusts a rich widow, but they

won't trust a middle-aged trust fund baby who's never married; or a man who married a woman too young for him or too beautiful or too overtly smart. The board trusts a man whose wife looks and acts trustworthy."

I'm such a good actress, my husband's reelected without contest every term.

Tonight, my husband will fine 12A $100,000 because their renovation has run six months past its end date; 6D won't be sold as an expansion to 6E because the mother in 6E scrapes the mahogany elevator with her double stroller. The more delicate matter at hand is whether Eddie Chang, a doorman accused of seducing 10B's wife, will be fired.

The only thing more unpredictable than a housewife alone in her apartment is a man who loses his job.

When my husband forced John into early retirement, he blamed it on budget cuts. When John committed suicide, my husband blamed me. When John came back, I felt forgiven. Every time John visits, I feel more alive.

———

I eat lunch on the terrace because the garden is always in bloom. My husband's mother was a horticulturist, which is fancy talk for "she had a green thumb." A canopy protects her plants from too much sun. Heat lamps melt ice. Plastic owls shoo pigeons. A mint bush repels rats. There is a library of enormous gardening books with her ball-point notes in the margins.

She wrote: *Don't use Folgers in rose soil, use Chock full o'Nuts!* She wrote: *Ferns pout if you don't treat them right— just like babies!*

As with the coffee grounds, I take her word for that. She didn't want her son, my husband, to have children.

She said to him, "This building's your baby."

She asked me: "You won't go to a fertility clinic? If something miraculous happens, you'll have it taken care of?"

I answered.

She nodded.

He nodded.

I did, too.

The next day, she gave me her gardening gloves. She confessed to me that if given the choice, she would have been grateful to be just a wife, then a widow.

She said, "Homemaking is so much easier when it's only you and your home. Take care of my home and— unlike my son—my home will take care of you."

My husband is cheap. He shouts. He doesn't like me to go out.

And so, I honor and obey. But I treat myself to lunch on the terrace.

Today's lunch is gyros and oregano fries. I always have

something delivered that I'm not allowed to cook. Tacos, egg rolls, fried chicken, fried fish. Stinky foods. Greasy foods. Foods I eat with my hands straight out of the bag.

Tony, the youngest of the doormen, says, "You eat like a bird."

"I eat plenty."

"No, not like that. I mean you eat like you're freakin' perched on a finger."

Tony sits on an upside-down water bucket and smokes. Doormen aren't allowed to smoke within sight of building, so I let Tony do it up here on the terrace. I feel bad for the kid. He used to be what you'd call "fresh-faced." First-generation Hispanic American, he had teeth like a toothpaste ad. Looking out my window, down over my gargoyle, I used to see him run up the block to help ladies with their shopping bags. When it rained, he'd run with an umbrella. When it snowed, he'd shovel. When the twin towers were hit, Tony enlisted. The war ruined his smile. He came back from Afghanistan a hollow, shifty smoker.

Then there were drugs: marijuana and heroin made him fall asleep at his post. PTSD gave him that thousand-yard stare. Then he stole: he told wives our husbands forgot to put cash in his Christmas tip envelopes, so we tipped him again.

The board knew we all couldn't have been so careless, but there was no proof. They wanted Tony let go and they wanted my husband, their president, to get rid of him. But it's hard to turn a veteran out onto the street.

Tony flicks his cigarette butt over the terrace wall and watches it fall fifteen floors to land in the private courtyard, where John landed it seems like yesterday.

"Heights." Tony shudders. "I don't know how the old dude did it."

"He did it quickly," I say. "My husband offered him a retirement package and John walked toward the terrace like he was going for a cab."

"Because you held the terrace door open for him?"

"You should have seen him, Tony. His face was so sad— sadder than yours ever was. He'd never married. He was married to his job. When he lost that, he lost his reason to get up in the morning. He was devastated. What he did, he would have done eventually."

"Except no one would have found him until he stank like an old peach."

I say, "It was cleaner for him to jump. Quicker. Quicker to clean."

"Says you."

"John's happy now. Everybody's happy."

"Yeah," says Tony, "I'm a regular laugh riot."

He picks up my lunch bag. He always takes it when he leaves. I don't know where he takes it, but he takes it because it's part of our deal.

He says, "When you're alone around here, you'd be

smart to bolt your front door. Stick a chair under the knob. That dude your husband's got on the agenda for the meeting tonight, that Eddie Chang, can get through your locks with the building's set of keys."

I say, "I'm the last woman Eddie Chang wants to seduce."

Tony says, "Seduce is a nice word for what he did."

"If he did something so bad, wouldn't he be fired by now?"

Tony says, "Thank the doormen's union for that. Before a guy's canned, he's got to be suspended, then put on a different shift, then switched to your side of the building so he won't bump into 10B no more."

"My husband's done all that."

"Yeah, yeah," says Tony, "but you and me both know how it works around here." He pats the cigarette pack in his shirt pocket. Winks. He says, "You make us too comfortable."

Years ago—when my husband found out from the super that Tony spent lunch breaks on our terrace—he questioned me. When I told him that given the space and opportunity, Tony—depressed and unable to be rehabilitated—would finish himself off, my husband got out of my way and let me do the board's dirty work.

I helped Tony overdose and held his hand until he died.

When Tony came back, I felt relieved. Every time Tony visits, I know I did the right thing.

———

For a week I've watched Eddie through my peephole when he delivers our mail. He steps off the elevator and stands in the foyer that services only our apartment. Our door is to the right of the elevator, and opposite it are a mail table and mirror. Eddie studies his reflection and mumbles. He points at himself. He makes a fist. He pouts like a fern. He holds envelopes addressed *Mr. & Mrs.* up to the light. Today, he turns and stares at my door.

He says, "Hello?"

Eddie is slight with a bowl cut. He looks as sexual as my wooden stool. I can't believe he had his way with the woman in 10B, but when he drops to his knees, crawls forward, and peers under the crack of my door, I do.

John says, "Would you like I should put a rubber whozeewhatzit on the threshold so he can't see your shoes?"

"He can see my shoes?"

Eddie lifts his head and presses his ear to the bottom of the door.

Through the peephole, I see his legs stretched out behind him.

His ankles tick right, tick left. He drums his nails (too

long for any decent man) against my marble threshold. He taps my door.

And then again, there's his "Hello?"

John says, "Your husband's mother would never abide such tomfoolery. Five minutes ago she'd be out in that hallway beating his ears with a rolled-up newspaper."

My husband's mother was a sadist. Well, maybe *sadist* isn't the word I'm supposed to use in this day and age, but I don't know what else I would call her. Control freak? My husband's mother was a control freak who wouldn't let her cook have a stool, her maid leave a speck of dust, her doormen forget their place, her son eat cookies in bed or marry a woman who couldn't pass her spot test.

She said to him, "Your wife will protect what's mine."

She asked me: "You don't scare easily?"

I do not.

I unlock the front door.

I run to my kitchen and wait.

I hear Eddie come in. I hear his faint "Hello." I hear his footsteps in the foyer, through the living room, through the dining room. I calculate the time I'll have to remove his scuff marks before my husband gets home.

The kitchen door opens and Eddie sticks his head in.

One whack of my wooden stool makes Eddie go down. I whack him again before he gets up. And then whack him a few more times to make sure he's dead.

I have to bake cookies for the board, so I'll leave the blood for later. I'm careful not to step in it as I move from my fridge to my cabinets to my counter canisters to the mixer. Eggs, butter, Quaker Oats, vanilla. The secret to keeping brown sugar from getting hard is storing it with a marshmallow. I put the first batch of oatmeal raisin in the oven and then return my attention to Eddie. I turn on my radio. Dismemberment and freezing are the priorities.

John fixes the doohickey on my jammed electric carving knife.

I work from Eddie's feet up and bag each little bit. Tomorrow I'll give Tony the head to take away with my lunch. The next day: a shoulder. Until evidence of Eddie, puzzled in my freezer, is gone.

When my husband tells the board that Eddie is missing, he'll be happy to report that another doorman problem has solved itself. When Eddie comes back, I'll tell him that my husband gave him to me to murder. When Eddie haunts my husband, he won't do it with repairs or errands. He'll scare him to death. And then I will claim this whole apartment as my own.

PAGEANT

PROTECTION

⚔

L isten up. We've got exactly four minutes before they notice you're not backstage with the other contestants. In eight minutes, they'll lock down the Radisson. In twenty, they'll issue an Amber Alert.

So get in the van. Hunch down. Take off your dress. There's a T-shirt and shorts under the front seat. Wipe off your makeup and take off that wig. Put on *that* wig. Stay down! Don't look in the rearview mirror. I can assure you, sweetie, you look like a boy. I'm sorry, but that's part of the drill. Remember, you asked for this and I'm here to help.

You can call me Aunt Mandy.

Here, take this Dramamine. It's chewable and tastes orange. It'll make you sleepy but keep you from getting carsick. These back roads are bumpy. Last year your friend, the Ultimate Grand Supreme Little Miss Savannah Stars and Stripes, refused to take her medicine and puked Mountain Dew across the Louisiana state line.

Yuck is right!

Hey, do you still suck a binky?

No? Well, aren't you a big girl! Breaking a binky habit is half the battle of relocation.

Relocation—that is a big word! It means change. Like when you change from your two-piece into your Little Orphan Annie outfit for talent. You contacted me because you want to change your life. You want to change mommies. You don't want to be hollered at to "Shake it, GIRL! Get it!" for the next eighteen years.

To change you'll need to do what I say and look like I say and talk like I tell you to talk. No more *y'alls*. No more *mamas*. We're on our way to New York City.

That's right, New York City! Lose your accent and no one will know you were a Miss Anything anymore. Don't and you'll be on the next bus back to Birmingham. I'm sorry, sweetie, but I'm not going to prison because you can't quit saying *cain't*.

Don't *ma'am* me. Ma'ams are a tip-off. A ma'am in Manhattan is like a dirty bomb.

The good news is: in New York City, no one will ask you to lip-synch "It's the Hard Knock Life" or burn your neck with a curling iron. Your friend, the Ultimate Grand

Supreme Little Miss Savannah Stars and Stripes, now goes by Mavis.

Yes, Mavis. It's a family name. A family name is how super-rich people tell everyone they're super rich.

How rich? Oh, sweetie, richer than Britney and the Doodlebops combined.

Mavis lives in a penthouse overlooking Central Park and plays center forward for her school's soccer team. Her do-over mommy, like all my New York City do-over mommies, got Mavis into private school. Private means it costs what your parents' double-wide cost to learn how to point to France on a map without using a computer.

Yes, that does sound hard, but it's not any harder than trying to tap dance your entire family out of a trailer park.

You don't want to go back to Serenity Acre, do you?

Okay then, I'll put my pedal to the metal.

Until you're placed in a no-take-backs home like Mavis's, you'll stay with me. I live on Madison, which is not as rich as Mavis's address, but is rich enough for me to stay home with you girls, who my husband tells friends are foster care kids. My husband is a magazine editor, which means his job is no more secure than a Pixy Stix backstage before Pro-Am modeling. He's too old to get a new job, so he appreciates the risky but lucrative business I'm in. *Lucrative* means good for you and good for me. Like a bouncy house! Girls bounce in and girls bounce out. To help, my husband does a certain kind of laundering for me and pays off our super, who finds it suspicious that all of our alleged government charges are as white as mice after your spray tans peel off.

When you run into Mavis, she'll be less glitzy than you remember. In fact, she'll be completely glitz-free. Her hair will be flat. Her face will be bare. Not even a tinted lip balm. Without pancake foundation, her freckles will mask the features in the glamour shot used for her police "Missing" posters. *You'll* be unrecognizable without your fake eyelashes and flipper. After JonBenét Ramsey, you'd think pageant moms would learn to take pictures of you girls when you're not all done up. But they don't. Pageant moms don't want records of you girls being anything but Christmas card perfect. They never expect their prize possessions to get stolen. Or in cases like yours and Mavis's: to get up and go on their own.

The whole point of relocation is for you to continue to think for yourself. Your first thought was that being the most beautiful girl in the room isn't all it's cut out to be. And you were right. It's hard work and it takes an army of pushers and pullers and toxic glue to keep you that way. And here's a secret: beauty cracks like a mud cake. To secure your future, you'll have to rely on your wits. Wits are ideas, which means they're invisible.

Like poots in a pool? That's right! See there, you are clever.

Quick! Where'd you come from?

That's right, you don't know.

What happened to your birth family?

Oh, tears are good. They'll shut a conversation down.

You've got to have brains to play dumb. Mavis is a shrugger. But you know what? She shrugged her way out of a genetic predisposition for childhood obesity. You two are smart to get off the circuit before you age out. I wish I had. It's the Ten and Over division that's hardest to place.

Placing an older girl is like trying to get people to take a cat from the pound. Everybody wants a kitten, which is you.

That's right: MEOW!

People think kittens are cuter than cats, and those people are right. They think kittens are easier to train and pass off as part of the family, and they're right about that too. No nosy neighbor is going to give you lip about a cute kitten in your apartment. They're going to say, "What a cute kitten!" and go on about their day. But bring a cat into your home and your neighbors won't like it. Maybe your new cat stares out your window like a ghost in a scary movie. Maybe your new cat makes dogs on the street bark. Maybe your new cat is too eager to fit in and rubs against people's legs in an uncomfortable way. Whatever the case, when neighbors get uncomfortable, they make anonymous calls. Anonymous means they don't like what you've done, but won't say it to your face. They think the older girl you've taken in is stolen or psychotic or perpetually in heat. They don't want trouble, but they want that older girl gone.

On the Upper East Side of Manhattan, you have to be blasé to blend in. Blasé means lose the pretty cupcake hands. Never sassy walk. Making eye contact with anyone and everyone draws attention, which you don't want anymore, so you'll have to quit it. Smiling like a nutcracker will get you sent to a shrink. A shrink is a doctor who digs through your head like a plastic trick-or-treat pumpkin. If he finds proof you don't belong, he'll pass you off to the cops. The cops will ship you back to your pageant mom, who—last you told me—made you smear chocolate on another girl's formalwear.

Yes, mommies can be bullies.

No, it wasn't chocolate, was it?

Bad sportsmanship is inherited like a cowlick. It's a little part of you that's twisted and nearly impossible to tame. So when you have a playdate with Mavis for potential do-over parents to observe you, you will play nice. If she wants to kick a hacky sack around, you will kick that hacky sack around. If she wants to point to France on a map, you'll say, "Bonjour!" There will be no princess dress-up because that is asking for trouble. There will be no TV because nobody wants to see you second-guess yourself when you see your pageant mom cry on a ninety-inch flat screen.

And she will cry. They all do. But you can't let that make you feel bad enough to go back. You made your choice to relocate and it's the right choice and I'm going to help you stick with it. Now, why don't you take a nap for Aunt Mandy? Go on, close your eyes. Dream, while I beat the traffic.

TAKE IT FROM CATS

If someone moves to make room for you, take up more room. If someone is looking over there, there's something to see. If somebody sneezes, run. If someone brings a bag into your home, look inside it. If you don't want someone to leave, sit on his suitcase.

Clean between your toes. Flaunt your full figure. Hide loose change. Even though you can take care of yourself, it's okay to let someone be nice to you. It's fine to take a nap on the laundry.

If you stand in a kitchen long enough, someone will feed you. If you're alone in bed, use all the pillows. Just because it's gorgeous outside doesn't mean you have to go outside. Just because you can fit into something tight doesn't mean that you belong in it.

If you trust someone, open yourself like a cheap

umbrella. If you want to be left alone, park yourself in a closet. If you want to surprise someone, lie in a bathtub and then jerk back the curtain when he sits on the toilet. If you're not interested, don't look interested. You don't have to chase every bird that you see.

MY NOVEL IS

BROUGHT TO YOU BY

THE GOOD PEOPLE

AT TAMPAX

My novel is sponsored by Tampax. It's the story of three generations of women and spans three decades. That's a lot of menstruation. So every time a character rides the cotton pogo stick—Voilà! Tampax.

My contract allows one year for completion of a first draft and pays bonuses for alternative product placement. So, I'll give one of my characters anxiety nosebleeds. And you know what's good for a character's verbally abusive husband's hemorrhoid surgery recovery? Something from a blue box that will make his toots smell like a My Little Pony.

My Tampax account manager's name is Lisa. She claims to be calling from Wisconsin but doesn't sound like she's from there. Every Monday she asks me: "How is it going? On behalf of Tampax, I wish to be inquiring."

Lisa's job is to make sure I hit my deadlines. Tampax has invested a lot in this book.

I tell her, "It's going great. Two months in, and I've created three apps."

"Apps?"

"For people who buy my book as an e-book—which will be everybody. The first is called Don't Look. It's for the overly sensitive. It blurs and turns the type red when a dog dies or a baby is born with a birth defect. Stuff like that. My second is It's Not Okay When You Say It, and it delivers an electrical zap if the reader laughs at a racial slur. My third is Jesus Thesaurus, which replaces explicit sexual language with church words. So, when one of my characters *saints* a guy's *disciple,* he'll beg her to *cavalry* his *Baptists* and *shout amen.*"

There is silence on the other end of the line.

"Lisa?"

"I am deciphering. I am also tallying the greater number of books that may be sold because these applications will widen your readership. Your husband will be very proud."

I say, "My husband's a ref with the WNBA. He's on the road, surrounded by oak trees with tits. For me to impress him, I'll have to sink a ball from half court."

Lisa says, "Yes, that would be very impressive. But writing a novel is impressive as well. I myself have had the pleasure of reading your first chapter and the description you submitted. If I were to trade my shoes with your shoes, I would write another chapter so that you will be closer to the finish of your novel when your husband returns. You could present it to him like a cake. You have ten months and two days to complete your novel for Tampax."

———

To generate buzz for my novel, I've created the following Twitter handles for my main characters. They are: @GrannyWithAGun, @MiddleAgeMartyr, and @Unclad Undergrad.

My characters have Twitter wars. They live-tweet court trials and reality TV, with a penchant for *Toddlers & Tiaras*. I'm online all day figuring them out, and Twitter gives me instant feedback if what I write doesn't work. It's the ultimate editor: if it's not retweeted, it's deleted.

Lisa calls and says, "To add to your follower numbers I am following your characters as the company of Tampax and as my own private account, which to maintain our professional relationship I wish to remain locked to you. Your follower numbers are low. They need to be in the five-figure range to impact book sales."

I say, "To build numbers takes years."

Lisa says, "You do not have years. You have a contract,

which it appears to me you have not read closely. If you do not turn in a partial manuscript by the half-year mark, there will be consequences. You have eight months and twenty-four days to write a novel for Tampax."

"I am writing."

"Tweeting does not count. You need to e-mail chapters as a PDF attachment."

I say, "I know I'm behind, but I'm working. I'm branding. If Tampax would retweet me, I'll get more attention and be forced to write another chapter."

Lisa says, "Force is a den of tigers alone with you in a dark room. Force is feeling the hot breath of those beasts on the back of your neck. And then the drool. And then the teeth. So very many teeth, you will beg for death before you can count."

"Lisa, are you going to retweet me or not?"

Lisa sighs. I know she is losing patience with me, but what does a woman who wears a headset for a living know about writing? I'm like a credit card debtor to her. She gets paid to get me to write pages.

She says, "Incorporate your sponsor, hashtag the title of your novel, and I will see what I can do."

The next day, @Tampax plus sixty-four others retweet @GrannyWithAGun for writing:

@MiddleAgeMartyr needs to buy @UncladUndergrad pants. DON'T GET YOUR STRING PULLED LIKE A

DUMMY. Right @Tampax? #TheStraightShooters
Daughter.

———

To capitalize on @GrannyWithAGun's popularity—she
now has over a hundred thousand Twitter followers that
include the NRA, AARP, and Miley Cyrus—I've leased
a water-gun booth for *The Straight Shooter's Daughter*
to travel the Southeast fairgrounds circuit. @Granny
WithAGun is the straight shooter for whom the novel is
named. The water-gun booth promotes the novel while
I'm working on it and keeps my most beloved character
alive with look-alikes.

The water-gun booth is staffed by retired ladies who
fit the @GrannyWithAGun profile. Targets are shaped
like oncologists and grocery shoppers with eleven
items instead of ten in the express checkout lane. Small
prizes are plastic water pistols with the title of my novel
printed on the side. Large prizes are plastic AK-47s with
@GrannyWithAGun's catchphrase: "Screw Gardening."

I follow the fair circuit in a VW Beetle with a Subway-
party-sandwich-size photo of a tampon on the trunk
and Tampax's trademarked terms "Anti-Slip Grip" and
"Purse-Proof" in Day-Glo letters on the driver's and
passenger's sides.

I video the granny barkers in their off-time screaming their dentures out on roller coasters, losing their

dentures in caramel apples, and styling their purple bouffants to resemble cotton candy. My videos go viral, and every time someone views one on my novel's You-Tube channel, that person has to sit through an ad for *The Straight Shooter's Daughter* that is presented by Tampax.

Lisa asks, "What do you call the prank where the old ladies throw knitted shawls over younger ladies wearing swimming suit tops?"

"Afghan-bombing."

"Oh yes, afghan-bombing. We have watched this video many times in our call center."

I ask, "What do you think Tampax would say about leasing a *Straight Shooter's Daughter* booth for the Midwest circuit? Where are you, Madison? We could get together and see who wins the blue ribbon for the biggest cheese wheel."

Lisa says, "I predict Tampax will say that expanding your circuit tour will stretch you too thinly. While Tampax is impressed with your efforts, you have been on the road for nine weeks. Your booth can run itself. Your grannies are capable. Besides, your publicity videos are doing the work of an army."

"Is it the gun control issue?"

"No, Tampax champions female empowerment. They are bothered by the fact that the popularities of your characters of childbearing age have not taken off."

"Give them time."

"You do not have that kind of time. You have six months and one day to turn in a novel for Tampax."

I say, "I'll get an extension."

Lisa says, "You will not."

"Well then, I'll quit."

Lisa says, "Never has a Tampax novelist quit. You would know that quitting is next in the line to impossible if you had done more than click the "Agree" box on your contract. From my experience, I am guessing that you read the first paragraph that describes monies due. And then you scrolled to the bottom and clicked the acknowledgment of deadline box. In between these markers were one hundred and thirteen clauses."

"What kinds of clauses?"

Lisa says, "Why do you not use your company car to follow your husband to where he is currently refereeing in Miami? Tampax will perceive this as a step in the writing direction. You can write in your husband's hotel room or by the pool. You may order a piña colada—as many as you like. Tampax has no problem with alcoholism."

I ask, "How do you know where my husband is?"

"The same way I know where you are. You are on a bench in Decatur, Alabama, watching a Tilt-a-Whirl."

I look around. Everyone is on a smartphone: ride riders, ride operators, moms with strollers, girls in groups.

A woman leans against the Tilt-a-Whirl gate and holds her phone up in selfie mode to put on lipstick. I see the frosty pink color in the reflection. I can also see myself. I look small.

I ask, "Lisa, are you not in Wisconsin?"

Lisa says, "Of course I am in the twenty-third state, Wisconsin, nicknamed America's Dairyland. Here, it is cranberry season and the current temperature is eighty-one degrees Fahrenheit."

I ask, "Then how do you know about me and my husband?"

Lisa asks, "How long have you used Tampax? Since you were fifteen?"

"Yes."

"Have you ever switched brands?"

"No."

"But you *have* had extramarital relations."

So this is what a cold sweat feels like. I was fine and now I'm sick. I've never fainted, but now I know I will. I'm clammy and boneless. I drop my head into my hand. My other hand dangles with my phone between my legs. I stare at the caller ID silhouette of my Tampax account manager. The faceless picture doesn't blink. It won't go dark until I answer. And it knows my answer.

I whisper, "Yes."

Lisa's voice broadcasts from the tiny speaker. "Then

there you are having it: the only thing women are more loyal to than love is feminine hygiene. As long as women use Tampax, Tampax is everywhere."

———

It takes me sixteen hours to drive home without stopping. I'm running on gas fumes when I pull into my driveway. It's dusk. I throw open my car door and don't close it behind me. The car beeps, my purse and luggage are still inside, but I race toward my carport entrance. I don't stop to chat with my neighbor who's been collecting our mail and who waves to me from my porch, where she's watering our plants. I jam the key in my lock. I wrestle the knob. I fall into my kitchen, and the wall phone goes off like a home invasion alarm.

When we bought this mid-century ranch house, my husband insisted we keep the landline. He said it was romantic. The phone is yellow and has a cord that stretches from the kitchen to the far end of the living room. The number is unlisted. My husband told me never to give the number out, so that when the wall phone rang, I'd know it was him, and only him, calling from the road. He said he liked to think of me perched on the kitchen stool, tethered to his voice. In the beginning he called me Birdy. He hasn't called me that in such a long time.

I pick up the phone and say, "Baby, I'm home now. I'm not going anywhere. Please, please forgive me."

But it is not my husband. It is Lisa. She says, "Go to the computer."

"What computer?" My laptop is in the backseat of my car.

Lisa doesn't answer me, but there is something in my empty house that feels definitely *on*.

The curtains are closed and the living room is musty, save for the scent of freshly watered pot soil. While I was gone, my ficus reached the ceiling. It looms over the coffee table, and on that table sits an open Mac Air. The screen saver isn't activated, so I know the keyboard was recently touched. A Vine video is cued up.

Lisa says, "Press play."

Miley Cyrus appears onscreen. Her boy cut is as bleached blond as a Wiffle ball. She sticks her tongue between two twenty-four-carat-gold-flecked finger-nails, waggles it, and then shouts in her hoarse Nashville twang: "We do what we want to, Gramma!"

She and her dancers have made a fairground grannies parody video in which they pile into a dunk tank and lose their grills. The grills look like goldfish, and Miley looks like a woman in her sopping wet halter top that reads: *S'up.*

Lisa says, "Miss Cyrus is lobbying to play @Granny

WithAGun's nudist granddaughter, @UncladUndergrad, in the movie adaption of *The Straight Shooter's Daughter.* To prepare, she has released a statement via Twitter that once the book is written, she will read the book."

I say, "You've been in my house."

Lisa says, "If Tampax can land Miss Cyrus as their spokesperson, they will be extremely pleased. Tampax has no problem with twerking. Miss Cyrus, however, has a shelf life for wearing Caucasian-colored plastic hot pants. Therefore, Tampax would appreciate it if you would flesh out the character Miss Cyrus wishes to play. Give @UncladUndergrad more to do in your novel. For example: she studies in the nude and she sleeps in the nude. She sleepwalks. And make her sporty. She can swim, play tennis, ride a bicycle, and go horseback riding. All of which can be done comfortably at any time of the month thanks to Tampax."

I say, "You can't special-order my novel."

Lisa says, "You should consider my special orders of great value to you. I am giving you orders that will be met with sponsorship approval. My orders are also helpful in regards to plot and character development. As your Tampax account manager, *my* order is to be of service to you. I want you to write a novel so that it may be published and make you a success. Your success is my success. And our success is the success of Tampax. I am looking forward to a first draft of your manuscript in one hundred and fifty-three days."

"A hundred and—that's nothing."

"That is six months. That is everything. That is more than enough."

I hear my car door slam. The engine revs. I stretch the phone cord to the living room window and open the curtains to see the giant tampon on the back of my VW Beetle shine like a Playskool Gloworm as it drives out of sight.

"You've repossessed my car?"

"We have."

"But, my laptop. My phone."

Lisa says, "You are speaking on a phone and you have a new laptop that is—as of . . . right . . . now—free from the Internet."

I hit the refresh button and the Vine video turns into a gray screen that says I'm unable to connect.

"You can't do this."

Lisa says, "You have enabled me to do this. According to the Terms and Conditions of your contract, at this six-month mark, if you have not turned in new pages, the consequences are as follows: no company car, increased monitoring, and a revocation of personal privileges."

I say, "I'll call my husband!"

Lisa says, "Until your novel is published, you will not see your husband again."

I barely sleep, but the next morning my alarm clock, which I did not set, goes off. I smell coffee from my Mr. Coffee, the filter of which I did not fill with grounds. The hall shower is running, steam rolling out from under the bathroom door. I open the door and find clean towels on the counter. Beside them are a hair dryer, a lipstick, mascara, powder, and blush. There is a dress hung on the back of the door. It's not mine, but it is my size.

I primp as I am implicitly told.

An hour later, my doorbell rings.

On my front step is a camera crew and the host of OWN's highest-rated TV show: *Novel Writin' with Paula,* which is sponsored by Tampax.

"Hey y'all," Paula says to the camera. "I'm here with a writer who needs my help desperately. Let's have her take us inside and show us her workspace. And then we'll have her show us her work. And don't worry, y'all, we'll fix her."

I've seen Paula's ambush show. It can be embarrassing for the writer, but Paula's tactics always work. Instead of dishing out ooey-gooey butter cake, for the past few years she's ladled tough love.

She says to me like she says to all of her surprised writer's-blocked guests: "Listen, whatever trouble you've gotten yourself into, I've gotten myself into worse.

And you know what? Worse makes for good reading. Novel writin' is just changing the names in stories you've already lived. And if you get stuck, make something up."

Paula has had three bestsellers on the *New York Times* e-book fiction list because Oprah and Tampax believe in second chances. Wiping her feet on my welcome mat, Paula looks like she might give me a lemon square and then punch me in the teeth. Behind her, nosy neighbor ladies come out onto their porches. They shield their eyes and stare. Paula waves to all of them.

She pokes me in the arm and says, "Let's get goin', girl."

She starts with my living room, where the Tampax-issued computer is still on the coffee table. Moving men come through the kitchen entrance and, at her direction, cart off the flat screen, the stereo, the bookcase, and all the books on it. Cameramen trail her as she tears through the rest of the house, rooting through closets and opening drawers. In the bedroom, she tosses playing cards, a knitting project, and something that the network will censor with mosaic pixels into a box. In the bathroom, nail polish and tweezers go in a plastic bag. Another sweep of the place gets rid of my ficus, my piggy bank, and a stopped clock. Anything I might be tempted to tinker with or be distracted by is sealed up with duct tape or bubble-wrapped for storage. In the kitchen, Paula takes my wedding photo from where it hangs beside the phone.

I say, "Please let me keep that."

Paula runs her finger over the image of my husband. He looks so handsome in a suit, out of his uniform of black-and-white stripes. I look happy beside him. I was happy. We both were. And then I got lonely, and then I moored up.

"Please," I ask.

Paula says, "Okay, it can stay. It can only serve as motivation. After all, that's who and what you're writin' for: your marriage, your man. You want him to fall in love with you again. Don't you?"

My tears burn, but I don't stop them.

Paula pats my back. She says, "I know. I know. It feels real bad, just awful, to disappoint the people you love." She looks at me and grips my shoulder to make sure I hear what she's saying. She says, "*And* to disappoint the people who are still very much in love with you."

I cry harder.

She says, "That's a good girl, admit you've done wrong. Now let's look at what you're workin' on and see where to go from there."

My new Tampax laptop holds all my novel files, sorted by date.

Paula opens the first one. She says, "Why, this is just

a big list of olden-timey rifles. You've got twenty-five pages here with lots of notes. Single spaced."

"It's research," I say.

"No, sugar, it's a complete waste of time. To write a book, all you got to do is write, 'The gun went bang-bang,' and then leave it alone. There are people who get paid to pick the right weapon and noise."

"Copy editors?"

"Sure, sweetie, we'll call 'em that." She opens the next file. "And what's this? Lawd! Look at all of this!"

"They're entries for my Amazon cover contest."

"Your what? Wait, let me get this right: you're gonna weed through all these—Lawd, there's thousands of them! You are gonna weed through all these covers and try and pick a winner for a book you ain't even writ? No. Uh-uh. I'll tell you what: I'll help you. Consider me your celebrity judge. Come on, I'll pick a winner right now."

Paula scrolls through downloads. I can barely make out the images whizzing past. The quicker she scrolls, the closer she pushes her face toward the screen. A camera-man chuckles. Her eyes must be crossing.

"There!" she shouts. She loses her balance and tips forward.

I catch her by the hem of her tunic and reel her back in.

She shows me an image and then turns the laptop screen for a camera close-up.

The winning cover depicts the backs of three ladies looking off into the sunset. One has a bun, one has a bob, and one has a ponytail. Their arms are linked and they are barefoot. They're on a beach and the tide is low. There's a dock in the distance and there is the shadow of a man on that dock.

Paula teases, "Which woman does he belong to, y'all? Is he father figure, illegitimate son, or mystery man from the past?" She winks at me. "I vote for mystery man, but we'll have to preorder the book to find out."

When we get to the book, there is only the one chapter. Eleven pages—3,200 words. I've got 125 days to write 76,800 more.

I say, "How did I become the girl who doesn't finish her homework?"

Paula says, "It don't matter. You just did."

She prints the chapter on transparencies and places the first page on an overhead projector that one of her helpers rolls in. I stare at my words blown up to fill the living room wall where my bookshelf used to be. Paula pulls a red felt-tip pen out of her bra and sets in like a surgeon.

She draws a line through the word *menstruated* and over it writes *bled.* Then she x-es out that entire sentence and the first two paragraphs about Middle Age Martyr and writes in the margin: *start the book with the granny, who your readers already love.* Two pages of scrap later, she makes a checkmark by Granny's line "Screw gardening, I got the rest of my death to cop a squat in the dirt."

She says, "Start here. Write three pages a day and you'll have a book in no time."

"But it won't be perfect."

"Sugar, nobody's perfect. And when ladies try to be perfect, their periods stop. When your husband comes home, don't y'all want to have a baby? You need to keep yourself in good health."

Paula opens her arms to give me a hug before she leaves. She pulls my head into her neck, grips both my shoulders this time, and pulls me to her so tightly I can't breathe or escape. She buries her face in my hair and pecks my temple for the camera. Then she whispers, "Writing a novel is serious business. You don't trifle with Tampax. Tampax is thugs. If you don't get to work quick, they'll chop your husband's foot off and make y'all blame it on diabetes."

———

Lisa calls and says, "One hundred and fifty-one days remaining, how many new pages did you write?"

"Six."

Lisa calls and says, "One hundred and fifty days remaining, how many new pages did you write?"

"Four."

Lisa calls and says, "One hundred and forty-nine days remaining, how many new pages did you write?"

"Two."

She says, "Although your daily average is four, your daily output is dwindling. What is the problem?"

"I've been living on coffee and cold cereal. I can't think."

Lisa says, "I shall remedy that."

Fifteen minutes later, the neighbor who waters my plants shows up at the door with a ham-and-cheese sandwich and a side of potato salad. It is a proper lunch. She says, "They want me to keep getting your mail. I hope that's okay."

"It's okay." I take the sandwich. It's delicious. Both pieces of toasted white bread are slathered with mayonnaise.

I write three pages.

That night, another neighbor lady shows up with a bowl of spaghetti and a hunk of garlic bread. She also has a blue Solo cup of red wine covered with a piece of Saran wrap. I thank her, write a page more than my quota, and wake up to cinnamon buns.

For the next six weeks I don't do anything but eat, sleep, shower, and write. My every need is foreseen and attended to. A neighbor lady cleans my house. A neighbor lady does my laundry. Two high school girls mow my lawn and trim my hedges. An early-developed fifth grader scoots along my roof and digs pine needles out of the rain gutter. None of them interrupt me, but they are always around. At any time of any day, one of them is in her yard within eyesight of my house: washing a car, filling bird feeders, tanning, practicing cheer routines, manning a lemonade stand, or rocking in a porch swing and cleaning a gun.

Tampax pays them, or really bribes them, to look after me. Once a week, an unmarked van pulls into the neighborhood, parks, and swings open the back doors. My neighbors line up to receive cases of tampons as if they're prisoners getting tossed cartons of cigarettes.

"Tampax is expensive," a neighbor tells me when I ask her why she plungers my toilet. "I've got three daughters."

Another says, "You expect me to use pads?"

Another: "Switch to OB? That's sinful touching. My church won't let me slow dance."

With eighty-seven days remaining, I tell Lisa: "I feel guilty about putting them out."

Lisa says, "Put that guilt into your novel. Perhaps Granny can feel guilty about Miss Cyrus's character having to take care of her in her old age. Perhaps Miss Cyrus's character moves in with Granny and Granny, too, becomes a nudist. Granny might teach her grand-daughter to shoot. Perhaps there is a shooting accident. Then the middle-aged martyr can be angry at them both."

I take all of my Tampax account manager's suggestions. I don't fight her special orders. I say thank you and incorporate them.

I write what's under my nose. If a neighbor lady shows up with Invisalign braces, I give a character Invisalign braces. If I have roast beef for supper, my characters have roast beef for supper. Except, one of them chokes. Or they all get food poisoning. And then they work out their differences while their defenses are down.

I make my husband the mystery man from the book's cover. The man is missing in the book because he's in the navy. I don't know what a navy uniform looks like so I make it navy blue. I make the man a captain, which I think is the highest rank. I put stripes on his jacket. I put him at the helm and surround him with mermaids. He doesn't succumb to the mermaids because he knows what it feels like to have his heart broken. Pirates capture him. Holed up in the galley, he hallucinates. His wife appears to him in her wedding gown and is remorseful. She promises never to hurt him again. She cleans his shackles and tells him stories. She shoos away rats and brings him a cake.

When *The Straight Shooter's Daughter* is published it doesn't receive traditional newspaper reviews, or good reviews anywhere, but the book is everywhere that Tampax wants it to be. The cover is printed on the backs of millions of boxes of tampons. It's laminated over public restroom dispensers. The title is on every wrapper. There are life-size cardboard characters at the front of every drugstore feminine hygiene aisle. Consumers can collect proof of purchases and send away for first editions. They can download the e-book directly from a discount link on the Tampax website. The hardback is at every airport. It's in every Hilton gift shop. Miley Cyrus has adopted the title for her MTV concert special, which of course is sponsored by Tampax.

There's no book tour and I'm fine with that. Until my husband comes home, I don't want to go anywhere.

Lisa says, "I am delighted to report that your book sales are nearing the seventy-five thousand mark. When they reach this mark, your husband will be allowed to call you and converse for one quarter of an hour. At one hundred thousand books sold, you will be blindfolded and driven to an undisclosed location where the two of you may share a picnic lunch. A reprinting earns you an overnight. A second reprinting returns him to you."

And so I spend my days refreshing the Amazon best-seller list, listening for the yellow wall phone to ring, and afraid to find out whose call will come first: that of my husband or Lisa, who on behalf of Tampax is requesting a sequel.

· A C K N O W L E D G M E N T S ·

Thank you to my husband, Mr. Lex Haris, who is my muse for all stories in which the husbands are good. Every morning when he brings me my iced latte and a doughnut, I know I am lucky. I am grateful and proud to be Mrs. Haris.

Thank you to my parents, a team, who are always rooting for me. And to my sister, Elizabeth Lawrence, who drops everything when I call and, like her podcast, is One Bad Mother.

Thank you to those who are always thanked: Mrs. Victoria Curran, Mrs. Koula Delianides, Dr. Elizabeth McGraw, and Mrs. Patricia McKenna.

Thank you to Martin Wilson, for margaritas and drunken book shopping; to Douglas Stewart, the best third wheel ever; and to Colson Whitehead, who reminded me that I'm brave.

187

Thank you to my friend and agent, Susanna Einstein, who shepherded me back into the book world (Gil would be pleased). To my editor, Jennifer Jackson, who drew hearts in my manuscript margins and made me open up more. To Sandy Hodgman, who introduced me abroad. To Clare Hey in the UK for letters and vision boards. And to John Fontana, who's covered me from my start.

Thank you to my book clubs, YA and Classic Trashy. And to poker players and bridge ladies.

And finally thank you to the magazine fiction editors who pulled nearly all of my stories out of the slush. You made me trust my voice after a long silence. Without your support, there would be no *American Housewife*. And this American housewife is forever in your debt. Cheers to: Laurel Coffey of *Blue Mesa Review*, David Daley of *FiveChapters*, J. Bradley of *Monkey Bicycle*, Randa Jarrar of *The Normal School*, Jessy Goodman of *The Rumpus*, Sayantani Dasgupta of *Crab Creek Review*, Tagert Ellis of *Faultline Journal*, Barbara Westwood Diehl of *The Baltimore Review*, Emma Carmichael of *The Hairpin*, and Allegra Hyde and Gary Garrison of *Hayden's Ferry Review*.

Many of the stories were previously published in the following publications· "What I Do All Day" in *Blue Mesa Review* (Spring 2013), "The Wainscoting War" in *Faultline Journal of Arts and Letters* (June 2014), "Dumpster Diving with the Stars" in *Five Chapters* (July 2013), "Hello! Welcome to Book Club" in *Blue Mesa Review* (Spring 2013), "The Fitter" in *Hayden's Ferry Review* (Fall 2014), "How to Be a Grown-Ass Lady" in *The Baltimore Review* (Summer 2014), "How to Be a Patron of the Arts" in *Crab Creek Review* (Spring 2014), "Pageant Protection" in *The Rumpus* (February 2014), "Take It from Cats" in *The Hairpin* (July 2014), and "My Novel Is Brought to You by the Good People at Tampax" in *The Normal School* (Spring 2014).

A NOTE ABOUT THE AUTHOR

Helen Ellis is the acclaimed author of *Eating the Cheshire Cat*. She is a poker player who competes on the national tournament circuit. Raised in Alabama, she lives with her husband in New York City.

A NOTE ABOUT THE TYPE

The text of this book was set in Filosofia, a typeface
designed by Zuzana Licko in 1996 as a revival of
the typefaces of Giambattista Bodoni (1740–1813).
Licko, born in Bratislava, Czechoslovakia, in 1961, is
the cofounder of Emigre, a digital type foundry and
publisher of *Emigre* magazine, based in Northern
California. Founded in 1984, coinciding with the
birth of the Macintosh, Emigre was one of the first
independent type foundries to establish itself around
personal computer technology.